THE BOY TRAPPED IN TIME

STEPHEN STERLING

CONTENTS

PROLOGUE

July 24th, 1969

"Again," demanded Dean Foster, whose face wore dissatisfaction like it would never go out of season.

"Really?" complained Phillip, himself frustrated at doing the same menial tasks for hours and days on end. It was ironic for someone who had been brought up to never use magic for basic chores to now have magic made into one. "I landed on the X this time. Can't I go somewhere else?"

"No, your *foot* landed on the X. You were supposed to have the X *between* your feet. It's strange that you have a strong intuition for traveling longer distances, but are sloppy when it comes to close ones. Again."

Phillip walked back behind the desk and prepared to teleport himself over the miniscule X. He was getting closer. The previous days, the dean had been asking Phillip to demonstrate what he had been taught before, and Phillip was more than happy to show off. Now, the dean was making him feel like an idiot. Phillip took another breath and teleported himself once again onto the X. This time, he adjusted himself based on his last shot. When he looked down at his feet, he sighed when he saw that the X was under his other foot.

"Are you tired yet," asked the dean. Despite Dean Foster's stoic facade, Phillip couldn't help but feel as though he was being taunted. *Was that a smirk?* "It's okay," he continued. "I myself might be this tired after failing so often, but I wouldn't know. Why don't we go out to eat?"

"I can take us to Winterburg this time," offered Phillip. Since the two were staying at Cardinal Key over the summer, the mess hall was empty, and the dean had taken to driving them to the nearby magical center for grocery shopping and the occasional luncheon. Apart from that, Phillip had decided to learn how to cook, and the current dean didn't mind his use of the kitchens as long as he cleaned up.

"Tell me Phillip, have you ever had the misfortune of teleporting into something?"

"Well, I once landed in a bush."

"And what happened?"

"The bush exploded due to the sudden force of matter slicing its molecules apart," answered Phillip mechanically.

"Where had your tutor been asking you to travel to?" asked the dean, who was unimpressed by Phillip's answer.

"Well, he would put up marks in various parks and fields and ask me to retrieve them. Kind of like a scavenger hunt."

"Open spaces, out of the public eye, risk free," noted the dean absently. "It's made you lazy, Phillip."

Phillip, insulted, started to reason, "That can't be the case. I have places that I travel to all the time: Psomira, my friend's house, school."

"And how often do you land in the exact same spot?"

"Well...," began Phillip, thinking. He was always thinking about how "off" he was when it came to teleporting, but his standard was never high. He always noted how he would land a few feet away. "I guess I do land *slightly* differently each time."

"Phillip," said the dean, with deep serious eyes. "I have something to tell you."

"Yes, Dean Foster."

"I have been changing the X by a few inches between each time you travel."

"No! You mean I could have gotten it?" asked Phillip, feeling betrayed.

"Actually, there were a few times when you would have gotten it. If I'm being honest, it was somewhat amusing for me, and you never caught on. That in itself tells me a lot about how you're using your aptitude. It takes more than mere mental calculations and physical sight. What if you had to teleport into a crowd of moving people? What do you think would happen then?

Phillip gulped, thinking about that bush and how it might have been a living thing instead. Mr. Wells had never asked him to teleport anywhere near anybody before, though he had practiced teleporting other objects and people with him.

"Exactly," stated Dean Foster, reading his solemn expression. "Well, we've already eaten out twice this week. I think we should make something at home for lunch, yes?"

After teleporting so much, Phillip didn't care. He was just hungry at this point. There was, however, a question bothering him.

"Dean Foster, how do you know so much about teleportation? Since I got here a few months ago, you always seem to know the answers to my questions."

This time, Dean Foster did smile, but it was not a mischievous one. Rather, Phillip recognized the same emotion that his grandmother might have had when recalling an old memory.

"Phillip," he began softly. "Does no one from your time talk about how I lived to my 300s?"

***

July 25th, 2024

This is ridiculous, I should not *be having to wait this long.* Carannog paced back and forth with frustration - no, annoyance - no, *rage. I am the second oldest of our group. I shouldn't even be having to wait at all to speak to Dido.* She stared down at her wrinkled hands - *so ugly!* Only very rarely did she let herself reach this point of aging - two or three times in her two thousand years of existence. *At least I'm alive. The non-magical girl and the haphazard ritual I had to set up gave me some more time.* As she finished her thought, the large and embellished wooden door finally creeped open, revealing one of Dido's slaves.

"Mistress Diana will see you now."

How much hubris does it take for one to don the name of a goddess? Disregarding the thought, Carannog shoved the slave aside and entered the stuffy, humid room. There were many layers of silken curtains that were blocking her path to Dido's throne. For a second, she considered incinerating them all, but chose to patiently push past them instead. *I don't want to waste too much magic on something so trivial - just in case I need it for later.*

"Ah, Cara," greeted Dido as Carannog approached her throne. Cara gave a short bow of her head - a significant improvement from when she originally was compelled to prostrate herself fully at the feet of her mentor.

"How are you?" snarled Dido. "I take it that events in America didn't go exactly as planned? I did warn you after all."

Carannog knew that Dido wouldn't be able to resist gloating, and she hated the smugness in her voice. Nonetheless Carannog knew that she had to maintain control of her thoughts and emotions, lest she give Dido an opening for a psychic attack.

"On the contrary, the December attack went according to your plans, but as for my own... I had to make some small adjustments."

Dido scoffed derisively. "*Small?* You call having to exchange a *magical* girl for a *normie* one to be an insignificant adjustment? Look at the state of yourself!"

She was being taunted now, and Carannog burned with... embarrassment? Shame? She only hoped that her dry skin wasn't reddening with mortification.

"You don't understand. That girl is more dangerous than we realized. She -"

"Than *you* realized!" interrupted Dido.

"She was different -"

"Silence!" snapped Dido. "I am still your senior and you will speak only when required. The problem with you, Carannog, is that you have been too stuck in your ways. You have been unable to progress, to adapt, to evolve. That is why I traveled all the way to your silly little school in the New World last year - to give you one more chance for evolution. Alas, you have always been incapable of seeing the bigger picture. Do you have any idea the kind of trouble you have caused me?"

"The December attack -"

"Quiet! The December attack was only the tip of the iceberg! You have been the cause of far greater failures! I see now that for the sake of nostalgia, I have been far too lenient with your disobedience. It's time that I -"

Cara had enough experience with her "mentor" to know where this conversation was headed, and it wasn't towards anything positive. Without hesitation, she preemptively attacked. There was no need for utterances or crafting a spell. After two-thousand years of survival, she could protect herself on instinct. With a slight curl of her wrist, the multitude of curtains spun towards Dido, wrapping her in a silk tornado. With a mere snap of her fingers, Cara ignited them. As she made her escape, she amplified the room with black, ashen smoke. She knew that she couldn't defeat Dido and her slaves by herself, especially given how weak she was at the moment. The smartest course of action now would be to run away as quickly as possible.

PART 1: THE TIME TRAVELER

I

CHILLS AND THRILLS

6:31

Perfect - well, nearly perfect.

Betty Collet, who had perfected the art of waking up without an alarm clock, slid out of the bottom bunk to get ready for the day. As she crossed off September 2nd, 1969 on her calendar, she glanced over at her roommate to make sure that she was still asleep. Normally, her roommate wouldn't wake up for at least another hour. Quietly, she slipped into the bathroom. Teeth, shower, change, hair, breakfast. By her junior year, Betty had her morning routine down to a science, and she could do it without rousing her -

"Why is it so cold in here?" chittered Emma, shivering in her blanket. She glared down at Betty accusingly from her top bunk. Betty, who was a thermologist, meaning she can control heat flow, was notorious for unintentionally transferring heat from her peers in order to cast her spells, causing a chilling effect.

"Well, I had to heat up the shower. Then I had to do my hair. I thought using magic would be quieter than using a blow dryer."

"And now you're hand-ironing your clothes," sighed Emma, climbing down. "I thought we talked about this. I don't like waking up to my dormitory turned into an Arctic tundra."

"I'm sorry," replied Betty. "I just want to have a perfect first day. It's our *junior* year! Arguably the most important year in our high school career!"

Emma couldn't help but smirk, even though she tried not to. Betty had claimed that each of the years would be the most important since they were first roommates back in sixth grade. "Fine, but I'm still upset. I'll forgive you if you wait for me to go get breakfast."

Betty obliged her roommate and in no time, the two were headed down to the mess hall. On their way, they saw a group of sixth grade girls being led by their mentor.

Emma scoffed, "In a couple of weeks, half of them are going to decide that breakfast isn't as important as sleeping in."

Betty chuckled, knowing it to be a statement of truth. For breakfast, she got a plate of scrambled eggs and toast while Emma had oatmeal and berries. The mess hall was atypically busy, but it *was* the first day of classes, meaning that most students were already up from the excitement of beginning a new school year. Betty looked around, but their usual spots were taken by middle-schoolers whose uniforms bore the scars of youthful magi who haven't quite yet learned how to properly use their new housekeeping incantations.

"This wouldn't have been a problem if you had woken up on time," teased Betty, noticing that Emma herself was on the lookout for a place to sit.

Emma didn't merit a response, but pointed to a booth. "There's only one person sitting there. Maybe we can ask to join him."

"Alright," shrugged Betty, curious who he was. Unlike several of her classmates, he opted to keep his soft brown hair short. Meanwhile, he was reading while taking a bite out of a piece of bacon. He was definitely old enough to be in high school, but she hadn't met him before.

"Do you know him?" asked Betty.

"Not well," responded Emma. "He transferred in the middle of the second semester last year, but he's so quiet and reserved."

"Excuse us," began Emma when they approached him. "Do you mind if we sit with you? Everywhere else is taken."

"Help yourself," he said, gesturing to them to have a seat. "Weren't you in one of my classes last year?"

"Yes," answered Emma, cordially. "We had cartography together. This is my roommate, Betty."

"Nice to meet you, I'm Phillip."

"Likewise. What are you reading?"

Phillip closed his book and presented the cover. "Folk tales from the Balkans. It's just some pleasure reading before the semester starts."

"What are the Balkans?" asked Betty.

Emma, who was a navigator, answered for Phillip. "The Balkans is a peninsula in southeastern Europe."

"It's where countries like Greece and Serbia are," added Phillip.

"Oh, like Yugoslavia?" asked Betty.

Phillip hesitated before answering, "Well, yes. That's actually where my dad is from."

"Oh wow, was he trying to escape the communist regime?"

Phillip gave her a stare that took a little too long before answering. "Y-yes. My mom is American, though. They met after he moved here."

Before they could continue the conversation, the bell rang, signaling the ten minute period students had in order to get to class.

"Well, I guess it's time to go," said Betty, always pleased to meet new people. "Welcome to Cardinal Key. I hope I'll see you around."

2

THE TAFL TEAM

Phillip watched a myriad of unfamiliar students trickle into the classroom, and he felt like he was in a foreign country. Even the uniforms were slightly different from those in the twenty-first century. Dean Foster helped him change his style a bit in order to fit in with the other students, but he still felt like a stranger in a strange land. Many of his peers were ignoring him, choosing to sit with their own friends. However, the girl he met just now at breakfast boldly decided to sit next to him.

"Hi," he greeted.

"Hello, I didn't know you were taking this class."

"Is your friend, Emma, in here, too?" asked Phillip, trying to make conversation.

"No, she's a navigator, so she's actually taking environmental science."

Phillip was just then reminded of his best friend Mark. And Aisling. And Kalina. And Mom and Dad. He stopped his thoughts from popping up before he became too sentimentally home-sick. *If I start tearing up, the whole school will make fun of me and no one will want to be my friend.*

He swallowed the lump in his throat and responded, "That's cool."

Just then, the bell rang, and the teacher promptly began the class. Phillip nearly found himself falling asleep since the lecture was so boring, but that was to be expected for the first day. The syllabus was useful, but it never made for an interesting topic of study. It didn't help that there were always students who asked the same insipid questions about the syllabus for each period. When the lunch bell finally rang again, Phillip packed his books and headed to the mess hall, one of his favorite places to be since it won't change in over half a century. The menu, the seats, the checkerboarded floors...

"Phillip! Wait up!"

Phillip turned around to see Betty walking up to him.

"What's up, Betty?"

She gave him a quizzical look as if trying to interpret what he had just said. Her azure eyes quickly glanced towards the ceiling before continuing.

"I was wondering if you've joined any clubs yet. I'm actually co-captain of the Elementafl team."

Phillip's own eyes immediately lit up. "You play Elementafl? What's your strong element?"

Betty smirked mischievously. "Why don't you come sit with the team at lunch and find out?"

Grinning from ear to ear, Phillip walked with Betty to the mess hall, talking about their classes (they had at least two in common) and Elementafl. It was clear to Phillip that Betty didn't want to give away all her tricks, which he understood. In the same way several magi like to keep their spells to themselves, Elementafl players liked to keep their strategies private as well. When they got to the table, Betty introduced Phillip to the team.

"Hi everyone, I've found a new member. This is Phillip."

The tallest student got up first to greet Phillip. *How weird? In my time, no one would have done that. He must be the co-captain.* His ruddy brown hair was kept neatly combed to the right and his clothes were perfectly ironed, a trait that Phillip recognized among many students in this era.

"Hello, Phillip, I'm Nicholas Whitesell, but you can call me Nick. I think you might have joined one of my classes last semester. Anyways, I'm co-captain of the team along with Betty. Here we have Sally Culper, Glenn Townsend, and Nancy O'Donnell."

"Nice to meet you all," said Phillip, and they all waved back to him. He stared down at the ongoing Elementafl game, which Nick was clearly winning. The poor freshman looked almost out of breath.

Betty saw it, too, saying, "Watch your aerial pieces, Glenn, that's how Nick likes to get you."

"You should listen to her," he agreed.

"But what if you're just saying that now to throw me off guard?" asked Glenn, repositioning his glasses.

"You'll just have to take a chance," teased Nick. "Phillip, please sit down. We're happy to have another member."

"Thank you," replied Phillip, setting his tray on the end of the table. "I'm guessing you're an aeromancer."

"Aerologist," corrected Nick, moving one of his electrical pieces.

"Are they not the same?"

"I prefer aerologist since it's the more modern term," explained Nick. "Besides, I feel like '-mancies' are more commonly associated with those ridiculous new religious movements you see popping up in places like California. We're not occultists, obviously."

Phillip was aware of the movement to change suffixes, but even in the future, people still mix up the two terms.

"What about you, Phillip? What's your aptitude?" Nick asked.

"I... prefer to keep it private, sorry" replied Phillip, who was a little embarrassed at his own awkwardness.

"Well that's hardly fair," commented another girl. If Phillip remembered correctly, that was Sally speaking. "He just told you his own, so now you've put him at a disadvantage."

"Sorry," apologized Phillip again. "The dean himself told me not to say anything."

"Don't worry about it, pal," assured Nick, with a smirk. "I'm sure I can beat you at Elementafl either way."

"Nick!" whispered Betty, worried that he was about to scare off Phillip, who was almost blushing at the confidence Nick exuded. He had a younger sister, though, and knew how to shoot back.

"I'd love to have a chance to prove you wrong," answered Phillip.

"We're meeting up later today in one of the classrooms after school," informed Betty. "You two can play against each other then! It's room twelve."

"I'll see you there," finished Phillip, who stood up to grab a bite to eat before the lunch period was over. He knew that he would be using a lot of magic by the time he started his private training with the dean, and he wanted to make sure he had enough energy to get himself through the day.

3

MAKING THE MATCH

Later that afternoon, Phillip knocked on the open classroom door, announcing his presence. Everyone had already arrived before him, and two games of Elementafl were already set up.

"Sorry I'm late. My last period ran a little late."

The truth was that he had just come from his private study with Dean Foster, who had spent the whole week drilling and testing Phillip on long distance teleportations, pushing him further then Mr. Wells ever did. Although it was a nice change from the mundane short distance travels, it was even more tiring because Dean Foster was much more focused on precision teleportation across long distances *without* calculations, saying that if Phillip were ever in danger, he would need to be able to teleport without having to plot out a trajectory. Phillip liked and trusted this dean, even though he claimed that he knew another traveler in his lifetime who could teleport accurately from London to Moscow to Canberra in less than a minute. Apparently this same prodigious teleporter needed only a mere sketch in order to go somewhere, which Phillip found hard to believe.

"No worries," assured Betty. "We only just started. I know you and Nick wanted to play, but he's in a match with Nancy right now."

"You can cover for me, right, Betty?" chimed Nick. "I'd like to test our new team member."

"Oh sure," responded Betty, who seemed momentarily flustered, but picked up on Nick's game seamlessly.

Meanwhile, Nick brought out another set of Elementafl, and Phillip helped him set up the pieces. Although his father had drilled him the game when he was younger, Phillip didn't practice as often during the school year, and he was afraid that he was about to make a fool out of himself. According to Betty, Nick's gameplay tended to be aerial, so Phillip mentally prepared himself for that. He himself didn't have a preference between any of the elements, but decided that a geometric or melancholic play would be a worthwhile countermeasure against Nick.

"You seem thoughtful," said Nick, moving first. "Are you anxious?"

"Maybe a little," admitted Phillip, who was starting to get slightly irritated at the provocations.

"Don't be," answered Nick. "I'll try to make the game short."

Phillip snickered and rolled his eyes at the smack talk, but he didn't let it be distracting. He couldn't let it be distracting because despite everything else, Nick *was excellent* at Elementafl, and it seemed that he was surprised at Phillip's skill as well. Almost a half hour had passed and the two were still playing. Phillip knew that some Elementafl matches could take hours, but by this time, the rest of the club had surrounded the two upperclassmen, watching them with intense eyes. It was move after move after move, neither of the two decisively able to gain the upper hand. Parry. Retreat. Fork. Trade. Eventually, Phillip took a hanging piece, gaining a small advantage that set the tone for the rest of the game. Although Nick held out the best he could, his magic began to tire out from having already played a couple of games that day, and it was downhill from there.

"I think that's mate," said Phillip.

Nick had just stared at the board, but slowly nodded his head in agreement.

"Good game," he conceded. Without shaking Phillip's hand, he began to pack up the pieces. "It's getting late, we should end for tonight. See y'all next time."

He left Betty and Phillip behind as the other three students had already gone to dinner.

"Don't worry about him," reassured Betty. "I've beat him a couple of times, but he's still a sore loser. I'm sure he'll come around. By the way, I'm meeting up with some of my other friends for dinner. You're invited."

Phillip hadn't had an opportunity to make new friends at the school, so he was happy to accept the invitation.

"Will Emma be there?" he asked.

"Why?" retorted Betty, with a hint of confused irritation in her voice.

"It's just that I've met her before, and apart from the Elementafl team, she's the only one of your friends that I know. She sat nearby to me in cartography last semester."

Betty's face had softened, and Phillip wondered if she thought that he was implying that he was attracted to her friend romantically. The truth was that he was just trying to make conversation.

"Oh, that makes sense," she answered. "I don't know, she might have cheer practice. Don't worry, there'll be a mix of both boys and girls."

Phillip was glad regardless; since he had time traveled he had felt alone, especially since people had spread rumors that he crashed a secret party, alerting the staff. Even though he was the new kid, the others already had established bonds of friendship. He was happy to be included.

4

A Grim Alarm

It had been a couple of weeks , and Phillip started to get his bearings once more. Now that he had been in the past for several months, he found his classes easier and his daily routine more natural. Unfortunately, due to the stress of finding himself in a new time period, he had struggled with his classes last semester. On the other hand, Dean Foster allowed him to do remedial work over the summer, allowing Phillip to take Calculus 2, which was his last class before his private session with the dean.

Although Phillip initially thought of it as private torture, he now casually popped back in Dean Foster's office with ease, where he landed directly in the box taped on the floor. He no longer verged slightly outside of his domain. With practice, the exactness of teleportation came as second nature to him. The dean himself seemed to improve, and began listing compliments.

"There's been a lot of improvement. I think you'll eventually be able to develop a sixth sense for travelling. You're probably not even consciously thinking about the accuracy as much anymore are you? You're also a lot quieter now, which is nice. Those loud whip cracks when you teleport were starting to get on my nerves."

"I feel like I'm going farther with more accuracy, too. Do you think that one day I'll be able to teleport to different planets?" asked Phillip.

"As long as I have lived, I have never heard of such a thing. If you did travel across the cosmos, you may be the first person to do such a thing," replied Dean Foster.

"I think that I may have already done something like that, but only once. There's a place that's referred to as the Archives. I don't know much about it, to be honest. I think it's like some sort of nexus point of time and space. I know it sounds silly -"

"No, it does not," interrupted Dean Foster. "You forget that I am a few centuries old, and I have known a few travelers myself. I had a friend a long time ago who spoke of such a place: a library, a museum, a garden. He claimed that it had contained all the knowledge of the universe. I later met another gentleman from Austria who apparently spent ample time there as well. He actually died a few years ago. It's a shame, too, he was very knowledgeable in his field and could have helped you much more than I can."

Dean Foster sighed and sat down in his arm chair, motioning for Phillip to have a seat on the other side of the desk. Phillip wondered who these two men were, as he had often read and researched on his aptitude, which was not commonly studied.

"I've never read about any of this, Dean Foster," he continued, mentally recalling the literature. "I'd like to go back, but I don't know how. Did the travelers you met ever mention how they did it?"

"Unfortunately no, but Aldous did take me there once. It was beautiful, and I will never forget it."

"Do you mean Aldous Norwich!" exclaimed Phillip.

"The one and the same."

"I read his autobiography. Apart from being a renowned traveler, his discoveries make him one of the most famous and influential wizards in history!"

"Yes, I suppose it does, but it will always be hard for me to see him that way. We were close friends once."

Dean Foster held a reminiscing look in his eye, and for a moment he looked like he was still in his twenties - *or would that mean in his one-hundreds?* thought Phillip.

"What about the other man?" prompted Phillip.

"Herr Flamm was... eccentric," claimed Dean Foster. "I met him at a physics conference, but when I had brought up the subject with him, he said that he could not and would not speak of it for reasons that he would not tell me. He all but confirmed his visit to the Archives."

"I wonder why that is," began Phillip, but before he could proceed, an alarm bell went off in Dean Foster's office.

The dean stood up, and with a flick of his hand, silenced the loud ringing. He headed out the door and motioned for Phillip to follow him. In the distance, they could hear the church grims howling.

"It's coming from the border on the Enchanted Forest," stated Dean Foster, looking out the hallway window. He placed his hand on Phillip's shoulder. "Take us there."

Phillip had sworn he had caught a glance of the umbral and canine features of a church grim before its spectre vanished and the howling subsided. The dean himself walked along the edges of the forest, staring intensely through the trees. Despite the myriad of questions that Phillip had thought of, he chose to remain silent. He did not want to disturb his mentor's focus. Eventually, the dean turned around towards Phillip.

"I could not see what it was, but in any case, I suspect the dogs will have chased it off."

"Can they navigate the Enchanted Forest?" asked Phillip. "If so, why hasn't anyone used them to explore it?"

"It's hard to follow a creature that you can't see. Although I am quite fond of them, they protect our school by nature and are practically untrainable."

"We don't have any in the future," noted Phillip, to which the dean responded with a sigh.

"I'm sorry," Phillip added quickly. "I know I'm not supposed to talk about future circumstances. It just slipped out."

The dean merely raised a hand to stop Phillip and said, "It's fine this time. When I first became dean there weren't as many laws as to the kinds of magic we were allowed to use, and I have long been certain that the church grims would follow me to my grave."

"Are they not already dead?" asked Phillip.

"They are in a sort of inbetween state," replied Dean Foster. "I won't tell you anymore since I don't want to encourage any illegal activities. Besides, the magic required to induce such a state in an animal is cruel."

"Could it be done on humans, theoretically?"

"Do not push your curiosity."

The dean and Phillip silently marched back to the main building together before departing for the evening, and Phillip was sorrowful that he had made the dean uncomfortable with all his questions. Just as Phillip found it necessary to withhold details of the future, so too did the dean find it proper to withhold information from the past. *If I could find the Archives again*, thought Phillip, *I just might be able to find the knowledge I want.*

5

THE DAME IN THE DREAM

After the events of the day: the English exam, the howling of the church grims, Elementafl practice, Phillip was far too tired to do anything but head straight to sleep. He had found it far easier to doze off in this time period - perhaps it was due to the change in diet and a lack of blue screens. Tonight, however, he didn't experience the slow transition to sleep that he typically felt himself slip into. Like a puppet on strings, he found himself being paraded onto a lifesized Elementafl board.

Is this what lucid dreaming feels like? wondered Phillip, who couldn't tell if he were awake or asleep. The pattern of the board was perfectly memorized, but the pieces were alive and moving. His heart throbbed when the flaming hair of the living pyral pieces reminded him of Aisling, while the melancholic earth pieces had the calm and stoic look of Mark upon them.

"If I were truly dreaming, then I don't think I would be feeling such complex emotions as nostalgia. This must be real somehow," analyzed Phillip out loud. Clearly, such deep analysis should be a sign of brain activity that wasn't typical of sleep. Nevertheless, the atmosphere was still thick with the reverie fog typical of a dream.

"Even though you may dream, who's to say what you see is not real?"

Phillip turned towards the aerial piece, who was a woman, addressing him. So far, none of the other pieces had even so much looked at him, though they were engaged with vague static motions.

He considered her question before responding, "Though I know a circumstance to be real, it often feels to me like it's a dream. Maybe the two states are not as well-divided as we tend to think."

"Perhaps," shrugged the aerial woman. "Perhaps not. To whose advantage is it to go solely where the wind blows?"

Phillip furrowed his eyebrows - her statement had been so meaninglessly absurd that he thought it was unequivocal proof that she wasn't a rational being. Maybe she was messing with him to get some sort of reaction.

"I do not understand your meaning," he said impatiently. "Maybe this is just a dream after all."

If that was the case (which he was not certain of), then he aimed to explore and to see what he could make of this odd place, wholly different from anywhere or any dream he had ever visited. To his surprise, the aerial piece followed him, but he tried to ignore it.

"My name is Diana," she stated, and Phillip realized that she would likely be sticking with him for the rest of his nightly sojourn.

"Like the goddess," noted Phillip. "Your movements on the board are not typical of an aerial piece."

"You're very analytical, but as you pointed out earlier, the lines between theory and practice may be blurred."

"So there are no governing principles to your actions?" challenged Phillip. "Wait. I *declare* that this is a dream, and it is *my* dream. I have brought you here, and the rules of this world must be under my domain."

Phillip looked around at the other pieces. *Why was this specific piece the only one paying attention?* Phillip wanted to manifest his will on this realm, but was unsure how or if he was even able to.

"And who brought you here?" retorted Diana. "It seems to me that you are not where you rightfully belong. You are out of place at school."

"I belong in the future," responded Phillip nonchalantly. He had no problem revealing his secrets to a figment of his own imagination. "I belong with my sister; I need to make sure that she's safe."

"And how will you get back?" prompted the lady.

Phillip took note of the color beneath his feet. Next to him was a water piece, boredom written on his face. In his eyes, Phillip could see his own reflection, and the world slowed for a moment. A translucent clarity overcame him, and he recalled all his travels from Manassas to London. He remembered his adventures into the Enchanted Forest, and his visit to the Archives. Most importantly, he could remember every detail about his movements. The feeling and the flow of his actions returned to him, and he felt that he could even map unmappable domains. Suddenly, a voice snapped him out of his hypnosis.

"Who are you?"

Phillip turned around to see an old man facing off with the youthful and sanguine lady. Rage colored his face, making it redder than the pyral figures of Elementafl. *Dean Foster?*

"I demand to know who you are, and why you have come!" he shouted, but Diana just giggled. Her laughter was as light as the element she represented. What sort of answer did Dean Foster expect from talking to the wind?

"Dean Foster? She's just an air piece," reassured Phillip, who was beginning to feel more relaxed in his dream.

"Look at the board, son, and count the pieces."

A preliminary look told all Phillip needed to know. He had been speaking to an interloping figure, who presently attacked the dean with an ethereal sword. The dean responded with his own, the pair battled, casting ancient and arcane spells that Phillip had never even imagined. He wasn't witnessing a fighting match, like Mark at a wrestling competition, nor was this the kind of duel that he learned about from Mr. Campbell. The pair before him sought to completely dominate the other, perhaps to the extent of death.

Watching the dean falter before the deceiver, Phillip decided to act. If this really were his dream, which he believed, then he should be able to use his own intellect to change the environment. To his right, he caught sight of a table with a replica of the Elementafl board on it, even with the figures of the dean and the mysterious woman on it. Phillip knew he couldn't defeat this woman with his limited understanding of dueling, but he might be able to outplay her. Analyzing the circumstances of the board, Phillip began to cast the pieces, forming an Edinburgh offensive directed towards the woman's body, and giving the dean a respite. Unfortunately for Phillip, a modern Elementafl board didn't have pyral pieces, but electrical ones. Diana took advantage of this, and played what looked like a modified Chicago defense. Fortunately for Phillip, he had recently learned that Chicago defense was a favorite of Betty, so he had plenty of studying behind him on how to defeat it.

"*Pluvia*," responded Phillip, moving his hydral pieces into formation. It was a risky play against the electrical pieces, but Phillip loosely hoped it would be a stronger match for fire.

Diana, who had appeared opposite to him, responded by manipulating air, and the game truly began. Every move that Phillip made was well matched by Dido's own, and after a while they entered the endgame. Phillip's pieces were slipping, several had been caught one after the other, and he barely kept his king safe. If only he could break one of her defenses, and get the king to escape her attack.

"Don't feel too bad," she scoffed, almost sympathetically. "You play fairly well, but I was there to help invent the game."

Phillip was in despair when all of a sudden, he was startled by the howling of several church grims. *This* seemed to be real, as Diana herself snapped to attention, and out of nowhere, one of the dogs leapt upon her. She responded by ripping its head off its shoulders, horrifying Phillip. Soon enough, however, they were surrounded by the rest of the pack, and Phillip was surprised by how many there were. Looking upon their fallen comrade, they all began barking, and growling.

"I suggest that you leave now," said Dean Foster, who calmly walked into their midst.

The woman seemed neither distressed nor amused, but with total apathy she walked off into the distance, her figure dissipating like sand in a storm. The dean put a hand on Phillip's shoulders, and looked kindly into his eyes. The dean's deep blue irises seemed to expand into a soft ocean, lapping at Phillip's consciousness

"Sweat dreams," he muttered, and the atmosphere thickened, with a tranquil rhythm leading Phillip into a soft and true slumber.

6

UNBINDING THE MIND

Phillip uttered curse after curse when he saw the time when he woke up. He barely had a moment to take a shower. Fortunately for him, he didn't have to run across the field to get first period. Hoping that no one would be in the bathroom, he teleported into one of the stalls (who would be pooping at school this early in the morning?). Although he was not prone to teleport around campus lest he teleport into someone, Dean Foster's training made him feel much more comfortable with his navigation skills. He glanced at his watch: 8:13 - still two minutes to make it to class, even though he already missed homeroom completely. Phillip brusquely walked down the hall, where there were a couple of other stragglers heading to their own classes.

"Mr. Todorova," greeted his statistics teacher. "You're right on time, though Dean Foster warned me that you might be late this morning."

"He did?" asked Phillip, confused as he sat down.

"Well, everyone's here now, so we might as well get on with the lesson."

Phillip found himself fatigued throughout the whole school day. He had been so hungry that he had eaten two different sandwiches for lunch and three servings of french fries. By the time he had gotten to the dean's office in the evening, he felt like he was going to burn away.

"Good afternoon, Phillip," greeted the dean, who was talking to another teacher. He motioned the teacher away and invited Phillip inside to begin their session. "How did you sleep last night? I heard you got to your first period on time!"

"I did, but how did you know that I would sleep in this morning?" questioned Phillip.

"Don't you remember what happened?" pressed the dean. "I was rather impressed with your ability to handle the situation."

"The alarm went off, and we went outside to check the perimeter," responded Phillip, who naturally remembered what transpired during their last session together. "It was a bit of an exciting day."

"And then you enjoyed the rest of your evening," sighed the dean. "And then you went to sleep, and then your dreams were being manipulated by an intruder, likely the same one who triggered the dogs. I'll admit it was clever of her to take a psychic route to avoid the grims, and I had to direct the pack that way myself."

The dean stood to clear off a small table of books, and asked Phillip to help him bring it over. Phillip had gotten used to the clutter by now - it was a sharp contrast to Dean Schulz's more orderly use of the office.

"What's this for?"

"You seem tired, so I don't want to push you too much with teleporting today," answered the dean. He had retrieved an Elementafl board, and placed it on top of the table, which was situated between the chairs. "I heard that you play well. How's the club going by the way? I'm going with you guys to your tournament in Colorado."

"Our what? Nobody told me about that! I can't afford to take a trip to Colorado! I have no money!" exclaimed Phillip - shocked about the tournament, nervous about his travel prospects, and excited about the opportunity to compete.

"Don't worry; I have had a few centuries to be economically savvy, and I like to take care of my students - especially when they're going to show off *my* school. Speaking of which, how are the others in the club?"

"I like them, but I feel like Nick Whitesell doesn't like me," answered Phillip truthfully.

"That doesn't surprise me," stated the dean as the pair set up the board. "He's a good kid, but he's always been prideful. You might have just hurt his ego, especially with Betty's interest in you."

Phillip audibly gulped, and opened his mouth to speak. The words stopped at his throat and vanished.

"Have you not noticed?" asked the dean, looking up. "Some boys are aloof, but I won't push the topic on you anymore. Now, who's starting?"

Phillip motioned for Dean Foster to take the initiative, and a relaxed game began.

"You know, I had a weird dream about Elementafl last night," recalled Phillip. "I don't remember everything, but is that what you were talking about?"

"Before we went off on a tangent? Yes."

"I think there was a strange woman - Diana, like the moon goddess. Is that the woman you were talking about? Do you know of anyone like her?" asked Phillip, setting up his defense.

"I've never met her before, but it's important that we start training you on psychic magic in case this happens again. It's not always the teleporter's strong suit, but we'll figure it out."

Phillip moved his piece before conversing, "The woman had claimed that she had helped invent this game. Is she like you? Old."

Dean Foster took a deep sigh, and said, "If you mean that she has lived a supernaturally long life, I have no doubt that this woman has. There's not too many magi who could best me or would be willing to try. However, my aptitude is extremely rare. Perhaps even rarer than yours, and the only other way to sustain life in that case is through the use of blood magic and witchcraft. It's totally unnatural and disgusting, and it has always been known as evil and illegal, even back millenia."

"Don't some healers use blood magic, though?"

"It's not the same! Healing magic is not the same!" clarified the dean, with an angry fervor that startled Phillip. "The way modern magical authorities draw the lines is that they ban certain types of magic altogether, but that has not always been the case. When I was a kid, it was not uncommon to find a magus who knew how to work with fire, or a healer who could balance the body's humors. There were rules on how these arts were to be handled, but all the magic practiced today is watered down."

Phillip stared at the board, waiting for the dean to move, but there was only silence.

"I'm sorry, Dean Foster," he began, but when he looked up, they were somewhere different.

"Don't apologize. I have lived a long life, and I have witnessed several events - too many of them," he said, but Phillip was distracted. The dean's office had dissipated, and they were in a shadowy limbo with only the illuminated Elementafl board situated between them.

"We're in my dream," guessed Phillip.

"Not quite," corrected the dean. "But we are on the psychic plane."

Phillip further examined his surroundings, but as far as the eye could see, there was only darkness. Somehow, the only place that was visible was the sphere of space surrounding the two chairs and the Elementafl table.

"Where did the bigger Elementafl board go?" wondered Phillip, remembering that there was a lifesized version.

"As I'm sure you are aware, dreams take place in the nonphysical realm. What happened is that this woman, whoever she is -"

"She said her name was Diana," interrupted Phillip.

"Well, Diana took advantage of your unaware state," explained Dean Foster.

"What would she want from me?" asked Phillip, perplexed.

"If I were a nefarious actor, and I learned that someone time-traveled from the future who potentially had knowledge of future events, then I would really like to know what it is that *they* know. Come, let's explore your subconscious."

Phillip still couldn't see where they were going, but Dean Foster took him by the hand to lead him. Although psychic explorations did not come naturally to Phillip, the dean had assured him that it was something that he could learn through training and practice. Now and then, Phillip thought he could see an apparition or a glint of material, but for the most part he had to rely on Dean Foster, who presently came to a stop.

"What happened?"

"We've arrived at something along the lines of a memory storage - where *you* keep your memories."

"Wait, we're in *my* head?"

"Of course. Where else would we go?"

The logic did make sense to Phillip, but he had just thought they were in the nonphysical realm in a generic way.

"If this is my head, why can't I see anything still?"

"Relax, and calm your mind. This is your own mental space after all," suggested the dean.

Phillip took a deep breath in and then out. Little by little, he could start to see what occupied his mind. It wasn't so much the feeling of clearing it, but letting his thoughts pass through him that allowed him to see what was beneath it.

"I can see more now, but it's like looking at my phone on the dimmest setting possible."

The dean wouldn't have known what he was talking about, but instead, he gestured to a desk that had a laptop on it.

"Well?" asked Phillip. "Is that where my memories are stored?"

"As I said, yes. I'd help you access them, but I have no idea how to operate that machine."

"Oh," realized Phillip. "It's a laptop. I don't know how much you want me to tell you about it, but it's kind of like an advanced computer."

"You need to be the one to use it," prompted the dean, who didn't have much else to say yet. He patiently waited for Phillip to work with the apparatus.

Phillip logged onto the computer, aware that his knowledge of where he was and what he was doing helped to brighten the space. There weren't any applications on the desktop, so Phillip searched for file explorer. When he clicked it, he found several files that contained different types of memories.

"What do I do now?" asked Phillip. "Do we have to go through every one of them?"

"Let me think for a second," responded the dean. "What you've shown me is incredible; this technology would be like having a whole library in your lap."

Phillip gulped down, trying not to reveal too much about the state of the future, but the dean leaned over further and continued, "I had a friend from a while ago tell me that he had this girl, a patient, who was an amnesiac. What was interesting is that her memories were stored on the radio. He told me that he had to learn all about radios in order to help her retrieve her memories."

"So then how do illiterate or blind people store their memories?" asked Phillip.

"I don't often go wandering in other people's heads, so I simply don't know," responded the dean. "In any case, I want to see which files have been opened most recently."

Phillip blushed and hesitated. He wasn't sure that he wanted to reveal his deepest thoughts to Dean Foster.

"Don't worry, lad. We aren't in long-term. I won't be finding out about who you have a crush on or anything embarrassing like that here, and I'm sure this Diana woman wouldn't have been interested in those topics anyways."

All Phillip had to do was click on home, and a list of recently opened files and documents appeared under Quick Access. It was surprisingly easy to tell which ones were opened by his doing and which ones weren't as there was a cluster of files towards the top opened under a specific date and time.

"Blue Ridge Exploring, Kalina Kidnapped, Dalton, DC Market Attack," read Phillip out loud. "Do you want me to keep going? I know you don't like to know a lot about future events."

"It's okay," assured Dean Foster. "I just don't know what she would have wanted from you. What worries me most is that she somehow got past me and the defenses I've set up. She must be centuries older than me."

It was hard for Phillip to imagine anyone being that more ancient than Dean Foster. He knew that Ms. Dalton was at least a couple of hundred years old if his hypothesis was correct, but up until now, the dean was the oldest man he had ever met. Finally, the dean grabbed Phillip on each shoulder and stared into his eyes. When

Phillip looked away he found that they had returned to the physical plane.

"That's all for today," finished Dean Foster. "Go get some rest, and next time we might work on your mental defenses."

7

EXPOSED BUT UNCLOSED

Noticing the time, Phillip could hardly believe that he had just spent the whole class period exploring the psychic plane with Dean Foster. Still tired, he debated on whether or not he should go to Elementafl. At the end of the day, he *had* to go, and he didn't want to give Nick the satisfaction of falling short or to disappoint Betty. First, he resolved to get a snack from the mess hall. Outside of meal times, there were usually beverages and snacks (and sometimes candy): chips, popcorn, etc. Phillip grabbed a bottle of peanut pop and a bag of rainbow fish before meeting with the club. He had considered making a bag of popcorn, but he was already so low on magical energy. Besides, whenever he saw anything colorful, he always thought of his dad remarking how American magi loved to use chromatic spells on every product.

To Phillip's surprise, Betty was the first and only one in the classroom, and like always, she was intensely studying an Elementafl game. She always carried the Swedish Elementafl Primer with her for reference, and Phillip was sure she read it religiously.

"Are we the first two?" greeted Phillip, tossing his trash into the waste-basket.

"It looks like it," responded Betty. "Nick told me that he was going to be a little late today since he has to do a task for the stoickee team."

"I didn't know he played. My sister loves stoickee," reminisced Phillip, who had only caught his mistake as soon as the words came out.

"How old is she?" asked Betty as Phillip sat down in front of her. The two began setting up the board, but Phillip fretted about how to answer the question.

"She's... uh... ten years old," he lied. "She'll start school in a year or two I think."

Betty nodded and began the game, giving no hint of suspicion. When the younger students arrived, she directed them to start a game of their own, even though they had an odd number of people.

"How late do you think Nick will be?" asked Phillip.

"I don't know; he didn't say."

"He doesn't seem to like me all that much," claimed Phillip, who was planning out a geometric strategy.

"Normally, I'd reassure you, but I think you're right. His ego is a little sensitive, and I think he underestimated you at first. Oh, speak of the devil."

Nick had finally stalked into the classroom like a wild feline on the hunt for its next meal, giving Betty and Phillip a sharp glance before moving on to Nancy O'Donnell and setting up a new game with her.

"Did you see that glare he gave us?" asked Phillip, who couldn't help but shudder. "If eyes could cut, he'd be a butcher.

"What's that supposed to mean?" asked Betty, giving a chuckle, and Phillip was glad that the tension was set loose. He himself wasn't sure if she was genuinely amused or if she was being flirtatious like the dean said. Maybe it was even one of those nervous laughs that come forth whenever one finds themselves in the thick of a semi-agitated atmosphere.

"I don't know. Just that he wears his feelings on his face," responded Phillip. "It's your move."

Betty moved her electrical pieces into the Chicago defense, which Phillip was hoping for. If he were able to hold his own against some ancient witch, then Betty's classic and predictable move should be a piece of cake.

"I've long suspected that he has a crush on me," she admitted. "But to be honest, I don't feel the same way about him."

Phillip's focus was torn between the conversation and the board. Although he found the topic awkward, he couldn't help but be interested in her opinion on the matter. Besides, he didn't want to push her away by dismissing whatever she needed to air.

"He's not a bad looking guy, I suppose," said Phillip, unsure of what else he could say. Sometimes, he couldn't help himself from saying nothing. "Is it the personality?"

"Yes, I think so," agreed Betty, who then proceeded to blunder one of her earth pieces..

Phillip allowed it to happen since she didn't notice it, and the two played until he captured her king. Betty sighed, and Phillip pointed out the mistake she made in the Chicago defense, which opened up a conversation about its advantages and disadvantages..

"I know," explained Betty, justifying her moves. "I was trying to bait you into a disadvantageous position with that hanging piece, but you didn't take it. Either you didn't see it or you were being too nice."

Suddenly, Nick stormed over and towered over the seated pair.

"Can we help you Nick?" asked Betty, trying to diffuse his temperament. His rubious face showed that the calm question carried the opposite effect.

Nick ignored her and stared at Phillip, saying, "I know you're a spy. I have proof. "

Phillip thought it was so absurd and funny, he burst out laughing. In retrospect, it was probably the worst response he could think of in the face of someone so delusional.

"A spy for whom?" countered Phillip.

"For Russia! For the communist," accused Nick. "People don't just pop out of nowhere! You clearly had to make a maneuver that no other magus could make."

"I was born in America, and I'm not even Russian. I'm only half Serbian," answered Phillip, who was wondering why Nick would make such bizarre claims. He was obviously hinting at something, but Phillip couldn't figure out what it was at the moment.

"Sure you are, but I know about that aptitude you're hiding!"

Nick finished with a shout, and stormed away, leaving Phillip nervous. He turned to tell Betty something, but from the corner of his eye, noticed that Nick had thrown something at him. Out of instinct, Phillip teleported away. He had no idea where he would go, but he materialized in the midst of a large aquarium. Plaques describing the aqualife bordered the submerged room, and there were intermittent shelves scattered around. It was peaceful, and Phillip wished he could stay in the coral ambience forever.

"It's not real you know," informed a familiar voice behind him.

Phillip turned around to find a young girl dressed in a stola - Lucia. But that meant that he was in...

"The Archives contain no life except us traveling humans. That's why nothing deteriorates here. The shelves don't mold or decompose, and the books don't get dusty. I tried to set a blank piece of paper on fire one time, but it wouldn't take. Then, I tried to set a scroll on fire. Again, nothing happened. "

"If the tanks aren't real, then are they like television?" asked Phillip, but Lucia only gave him a perplexed look. *Of course she wouldn't know what those are*, remembered Phillip. She would have been born over sixteen hundred years before cameras were invented. They both sat in silence for a while, staring at the marine life, when Phillip finally saw through the illusion.

"That one fish repeated his swimming cycle," he claimed, still astonished at how realistic the scene was. Apart from that hint of manufactured beauty, he couldn't determine whether it was a video, a hologram, or some sort of technical advancement that he would never live to see.

"They all eventually do that. Their motions are really just meant to show their anatomy and behaviors and such," affirmed Lucia, whose tone was so calm and unearthly, Phillip wondered how often she interacted with other people. "The larger ones tend to have a longer circuit. I do not know why that is."

"What are you doing here?" asked Phillip, turning his attention to the youthful Roman.

"I like to come down here sometimes because it's so peaceful, and I don't normally find others down here. You travelers tend to be landpeople. What are *you* doing here?" she returned.

"I came here by accident, but I've been trying to come back for a while. Is Septimus around? I have some questions for him."

"I'm sure a version of him is around here somewhere," she said with a shrug.

"A *version*," repeated Phillip, as the two made their way down the meandering aquarium. "What does that mean?"

"He regularly goes back to Earth," explained Lucia. "And since The Archives exist outside the bounds of time and space, I sometimes experience Septimus out of chronological order."

"That must be complicated," noted Phillip.

"Not really. I have learned to perceive when he is from, and when I cannot, I ask him to tell me."

"Well that brings up another question," began Phillip, who jumped as a large shark sped by. His reaction seemed to have amused Lucia. "I also traveled through time."

Lucia didn't respond at first, but just gave him a look.

"Repeat again, please. Sometimes the transmission of language in this realm does not always work accurately."

Phillip specified, "I accidentally traveled through time into the past - before I was even born."

Lucia scoffed, "No you did not."

"What do you mean 'I did not?' I can see it with my own eyes! I'm living it!"

"I am not saying you are lying, just that you are likely deceived or there has been an illusion cast on you. Perhaps a sort of dream spell. Time-travel to the past is impossible because matter cannot occupy two places at once. However, if you disagree with me, then you can ask Septimus."

"If we can find him," sighed Phillip, who doubted that Lucia would be able to find her friend in the endless ocean of information.

"One of him likes to hang around in the coral reefs section. It should be the next turn or two."

"How long did it take you to be able to navigate this place? Isn't it infinite?"

"Sometimes," answered Lucia, who didn't seem to be bothered by the existential question that daunted Phillip himself. "But I have time, and I do not know all of it - only a sliver.

On the next turn, they entered a brighter space, designed after the coral reefs of Australia. On a sofa sat the elderly man that Phillip had previously met.

"Hello, Septimus," greeted Phillip, and the Roman turned around to examine him. Despite maintaining his old age, Phillip could perceive that this was a younger emanation of the learned man, with tighter skin and brighter eyes. *If this were the case, then why did I have to reintroduce himself in the past?* pondered Phillip, who found the paradoxical nature of the Archives frustrating

"He's met you before, and he has some questions," clarified Lucia, and understanding dawned on his face.

The paradox of meeting someone for the first time twice nearly caused Phillip a headache, but he chose not to think about it. If there's anything he learned from his temporal excursions was that sometimes you don't need to know why things are to know that they simply *are*.

"I see, why don't you have a seat," offered Septimus.

Phillip and Lucia settled on the plush pink armchairs across from each other while Septimus put down his tome.

"It's nice, isn't it. We don't have anything like it in Rome."

"The aquarium?"

"We have piscinae, but I mean the couches," chuckled Septimus. "Now, what is it you want to talk about?"

"Well there are two things. First, I want to know how I can repeatedly return to the Archives," requested Phillip.

"That's easy," responded Septimus. "How did you get here this time and the time before?"

"I don't know," admitted Phillip.

"That is the answer," confirmed Septimus.

Philip was always a little frustrated at this kind of dialect, but tried to give the answer some thought.

"Do you mean that I have to have no place in mind to go to?"

"Not even the Archives itself," continued Septimus. "It is a contradiction that this place is nowhere. Our best theory as of right now is that it is a manifestation of knowledge itself, but I am certain Lucia has already explained that to you. You see, it's very Socratic that the path to wisdom is recognizing that you have none. Now, what is your next question?"

"I traveled through time into the past."

It wasn't so much of a question but a statement that was meant to open up the conversation. At this point, Phillip was happy to take whatever information there was to receive. However, the Romans' body language implied that he would be returning to school empty handed. Septimus, whose light eyes seemed to fade with perplexity, glanced at Lucia, who nodded her head slowly to confirm that he heard Phillip correctly.

"If what you say is veritable, then I cannot help you. As far as I am aware, this should not even be a possibility. However, if what you say is false - a trick or misinterpretation - then it is likely that you have been deceived through witchcraft or sorcery. Here," he stated, pulling a scroll from between the couch cushions.

"*Protection from Fantastical Crafts*," read Phillip. *At least they didn't think I was lying*, he thought to himself. At the very least, it couldn't hurt to give their suggestion a shot.

"Read through it," suggested Septimus. "It will help you determine whether or not you are in fact under the influence of a malevolent enchantress."

Phillip looked down at the book and read the contents, but when he was about to ask Septimus another question, there was only an empty sofa.

"He goes away," said Lucia, like it was just a matter of fact.

"The first chapter has a list of questions that I need to answer in the state that I'm in. Can I write them down and bring a piece of paper with me?"

Lucia shook her ahead.

"Everything from here stays here," she stated. "You'll have to memorize them, but don't worry. You have all the time and more when you're in the Archives."

She finished and got up to leave.

"Where are you going?" asked Phillip, who didn't want to be alone in the Archives. It gave him a small sense of apeirophobia - fear of the infinite.

"To look at the whales," she said, either ignoring the discomfort in his voice or not realizing it. "I like the sounds they make. I'm sure you remember how to get back."

Ending the conversation, Lucia left Phillip behind to concentrate on the book. Time here did not seem to take as long as it did on Earth, and Phillip found it slightly easier to concentrate on reading without having to combat several minute distractions. When he finally finished the book and felt confident that he could perfectly recall the diagnostic questions, he made his way back to school.

8

A BREATH OF FRESH AIR

Everything was exactly as he left it, as though no time had passed. When he entered the classroom, the sun's rays were still falling, Nick was still standing, and everyone turned to look at him with their mouths ajar.

"You're a traveler!" gasped Betty, whose face shone forth with both pleasure and shock.

"I knew it! You must have traveled here from the Eastern Block!" accused Nick.

"Do you really think Dean Foster could be tricked by a teenage spy?" retorted Betty, who herself was awestruck at the ridiculousness of Nick's theory. It made Phillip's aptitude seem mundane in contrast.

On the other hand, Phillip didn't care about the situation anymore. For his teammates, everything was just as it was, but Phillip had spent what felt like hours in the Aquarium. Before he could forget the diagnostic questionnaire for psychosis, he turned around and exited.

Question 1: *Is my perception of space and time consistent?*

This was a tricky one for Phillip having just left the Archives, a place that existed outside time and space. However, the way time flowed when he was not there was "consistent," so the answer to that is 'yes.' Phillip entered another empty classroom and sat down on one of the chairs, looking outside the window.

Question 2: *Are any of my senses contradicting one another?*

Phillip pinched himself on the arm, then rubbed it. The book recommended testing each of the five senses, so he closed his eyes and listened to the world around him. The door to the classroom creaked open, and he was not at all surprised to see Betty entering. He had never paid attention to the scented lotion she wore, but he smelled notes of vanilla and honey. As always, she kept her blond hair in a pony tail all day, reminding Phillip of how his own sister liked it.

"I saw you pinch yourself," she said. "Are you wondering if this is a dream?"

"No, well maybe," admitted Phillip, certain that Septimus was wrong. Phillip recalled the manufactured dream he had undergone several nights ago and was certain that what he was experiencing now was real.

"What Nick did was wrong," continued Betty, pulling up a chair next to Phillip. "I can only guess why he's acting like this. If it makes you feel any better, everyone thinks he's crazy - even the middle-schoolers."

"He's jealous, of course," responded Phillip, shoving his hands into his pockets. "Which is frustrating because I thought he was a cool guy when I first met him, and I wanted us to be friends."

"I'm sorry," began Betty, but Phillip continued before she could.

"He's going to tell everyone he knows. I have to find Dean Foster."

Now that the cat was out of the bag, Phillip chose to teleport himself directly into Dean Foster's office, choosing to make his materialization as loud as possible. Fortunately, the dean was sitting at his desk alone, examining several sheets of paper.

"You do know I have a timeline for other responsibilities that I have to deal with," stated the dean without looking up.

"The chess club has found out about my aptitude. Nicholas Whitesell threw something at me, and then I teleported by instinct."

Much to Phillip's ire, the dean just shrugged and continued to sign the documents in front of him.

"That's it? You're not going to say anything? You're not even upset with me or Nick Whitesell?"

The dean put his pen down and addressed his student. "It couldn't have been kept secret indefinitely, but I'll talk to Nicholas. I'm sorry that he's been giving you a hard time. Where did you go?"

"Does that even matter?" retorted Phillip. If the dean hadn't been so uninterested in the first place, Phillip would have been more forthcoming with the whole story. This hidden pettiness would need to suffice for now, though, and he would to the dean about the sojourn later.

"I suppose not," said the dean, smug in his own ignorance. He clearly did not want to play into whatever game Phillip had going on with himself, which only frustrated Phillip more.

"Well, I'm sorry to be such a nuisance!" snapped Phillip.

"Hold on -"

But it was too late, Phillip had teleported away before he could hear whatever the dean had to say. It was only a matter of time before the enormity of everything got to him. The 60s were fun, sure, but it wasn't home. If only he were a spy, then he would be able to handle the situation better. Phillip chuckled at the thought - what he was so upset about just a moment before was now something he yearned for. He could always find humor in irony, and he took the moment of levity to collect himself.

The fresh air itself calmed his senses, and he finally realized that he traveled to the Manassas Battlefield - another irony: nostalgia for the future. Before he could feel overwhelmed, he decided to kneel in prayer. Whether or not anything tactile came from the action, he often found it to be an appropriate method to reframe the cause of his anxieties. Tonight, that meant time-travel, Elementafl, the tournament, and even smaller things like classes. He would and could eventually figure all these things out - starting with winning in the cross-scholastic competition coming up.

9
TIMERS AND TENSION

"Have you ever been on a skyship before?" asked Phillip, taking a sip of his sweet corn ptisane while gazing over the railing to the vast sea of space before him.

"Once, when I was very little," responded Betty, who herself was enchanted by the myriad of clouds before them. "I was excited when Dean Foster told us he got us tickets. He certainly likes to spoil his students."

"I can't believe the school paid for this," said Glenn.

"It wasn't the school," explained Betty. "Dean Foster is a lot richer than we know, but I guess it's easy to build wealth when you live for hundreds of years."

"Cool, I'm going to get more peanut pop."

The younger boy abruptly turned on his toes and dashed to the bar, leaving Phillip to endearingly wonder how much sugar he had already consumed. On the other hand, Betty was sipping on butter-spice - a richer and sweeter drink then Phillip's.

"I'm getting cold," announced Betty. "Why don't we head down?"

The two made their way downstairs to the interior of the ship where there was a lounge. Light radiating from an orderly array of portholes illuminated the space, and Betty chose a spot where the sun could shine on her back. On the other side of the room, Phillip spotted Nancy and Sally engrossed in a conversation with Dean Foster, who enjoyed recounting his many personal stories that have been acquired throughout his lengthy and interesting life. However, Nicholas was nowhere to be found. He was probably in his room studying Elementafl.

"Are you nervous?" asked Betty.

"About the tournament? I don't think so," replied Phillip. If he were honest with himself, he was thinking about how much he would miss his new friends when he finally returned home. He had no idea how to explain this to Betty or if he even should.

"I hate to pry," she began, which made Phillip's heart drop a little. "But how exactly does your aptitude work? And why did you start school in the middle of the year last year? I don't actually think you're some communist spy or changeling; I'm just curious."

Phillip took a large sip of his salty-sweet drink and took a moment to conceive of the best way to satisfy his friend's query without giving away too much information.

"The new discovery of my aptitude made it necessary for me to find specialized help," muttered Phillip, who felt dirty for using quasi-deceptive language. He didn't technically lie; time-travel *was* a new discovery of his aptitude.

Betty sighed in resignation, "I reckon that's the most I'm going to get out of you."

Without knowing why, Phillip apologized. He didn't think he had a reason to, but after the kindness Betty had shown, he felt guilty about keeping his secrets.

"I asked Dean Foster to take us to see the mystery cave system in the Rocky's," continued Betty, changing the subject. "Obviously we can't go all the way in, but there are places we can explore."

"Solid ground sounds pretty nice right now. I've enjoyed the skyship, but I'm also glad we're landing soon. I wonder where those caves go," mused Phillip, who had traveled to Colorado before to visit his uncle, but never did much sight-seeing.

"Some scholars think that they lead to other worlds - or potentially to some sort of underworld if you're a mystic type. Do you think you could teleport into or out of there?"

"If they did go to other worlds, it would be out of my current reach."

"In any case," said Betty. "I'm going to go back to my room to make sure my stuff is packed. You're probably avoiding Nick, but you should do a little bit of studying before tomorrow morning."

Phillip looked down at the Colorado landscape, and in the distance he could see the Rockies. They were... rocky. Betty was right, and it wouldn't do Phillip any good if he lost because of a grudge against a classmate.

***

Nick was helping Glenn tie a Windsor knot while Phillip's trembling fingers struggled to make his own. Despite having encountered a literal dragon, Phillip found the prospect of making a fool out of himself slightly more nerve-racking. Yesterday, he had put on a brave face for the sake of Betty, but now that the time had come, he was getting butterflies. Inwardly, he could hear every blood cell rush through his veins. Of course he could go to the Archives and spend an indefinite amount of time studying every possible maneuver for the game, but he'd rather just get the day over with. The three students headed downstairs for the continental breakfast, but Phillip could only bring himself to drink some tea and sugar before the tournament started. He had always felt that a full stomach tended to slow him down.

At precisely 8:15, Dean Foster showed up with Betty, who was wearing a deep, burgundy blouse with a mahogany skirt, in order to wish everyone luck and hand out the timers. As Phillip silently took his, he noticed a familiar woman from across the room and was unable to take his eyes off her.

"Phillip?" prompted Dean Foster. "The tournament's about to begin; you have to go."

"But that woman. I know her, she's from my -"

"We'll talk about it after. Focus on the tournament right now!" commanded Dean Foster, and Phillip, flush with confusion and anger, obeyed. Even from a logical standpoint, he could not just confront Ms. Dalton out of the blue. How could he accuse her of something that she *will* do? People would think he was crazy, so Phillip resigned to finding justice in his own time. Besides, it's too late now to escape to the Archives for a minute to think. All eyes were on him, and the game must begin without any sort of fishy business.

Phillip sat across from the first student, a boy from Mexico, and they agreed to use his own timer. Though he was distracted by Dalton's presence, Phillip had found him easy enough to beat. Never before had Phillip felt grateful for his father drilling him ruthlessly in what used to seem like a silly board game.

Piece after piece, Phillip kept up a high win rate and was feeling rather pleased with himself until he sat down before a girl with a navy and bronze uniform, and a fleur-de-lis crest, the emblem of Academie de Champlain. With a thick French accent, she smiled and said, "hello" before hitting the timer, signaling for Phillip to move first. He decided to go with an electrical pawn's opening and was stung when his fingers touched the piece. It wasn't uncommon for an Elementafl piece to feel like its own element, but this felt more like a prick than a shock. Phillip examined his pointer finger and though there was no blood, he imagined a sensation not unlike Mendicol.

"Ze timer?" the girl reminded him, and Phillip quickly pressed the switch so that she would play. Although he noted that she started with a terric defense (not an uncommon strategy to counter electricity), he was distracted by examining the piece he first moved and was reminded by the ten questions he had memorized to determine whether or not he was under an illusion. *Question 2: Are any of my senses contradicting one another?* For a second, the piece shimmered, but when the girl pressed the switch, he was brought out of his thoughts and focused on the game.

Unfortunately, his momentary distractions were enough for his opponent to get the edge over him, and he sustained his first loss in the tournament. It was quite the blow to his self esteem as he lost by running out of time (not that he would have won had he not been thinking about his finger). Nonetheless, he continued to play strong in his proceeding matches, when several students started to become significantly better than average. Despite this he pushed with fortitude to the end, earning a 1734 Elo, an exceptionally good ranking in Elementafl, and coming in sixth place overall.

The dean himself was highly pleased with his school's performance - each member of the club had placed in the top third, with Nicholas coming in second and Betty coming in fifth. Dean Foster, who was always looking for an excuse to splurge on his students, took them to a notable magus restaurant carved into the Rocky Mountains for dinner.

10

An Intellectual Introduction

This week had been the most clement and relaxing one that Phillip got to experience since the Elementafl tournament. The club decided to take a break for a couple of weeks since they had been working so hard, and some of the members needed to catch up on their actual schoolwork. Phillip himself had taken the rest period to spend more time outside. He had never excelled at tennis as well as his sister, but he knew how to play a decent game. Moreover, practicing allowed him to reminisce about Kalina, and he hoped that she was doing fine. Although he wasn't sure that she and the others were able to escape without him to teleport them away, he had to believe for his own sanity that they did. As he struck the ball over and over again, he smiled to himself when he remembered his observation that Kalina had an uncanny habit about knowing where the ball was going to go before he hit it, never considering it to be a result of her prescient aptitude.

The bell had finally rung, signaling for Phillip that it was time to go back to his dorm to take a shower before his session with the dean. Dean Foster had asked to replace their training period with an hour after school, which Phillip happily obliged. It let him spend time by himself, making the entire campus his personal playground as everyone else still had class. Since Nicholas had revealed to everyone his aptitude, Phillip no longer felt any qualms about teleporting around school, which made travel a lot more convenient. He quickly freshened up before heading to Dean Foster's office. As soon as he landed, a woman yelped, which in turn startled him.

"I'm sorry," Phillip said. He was so embarrassed his rapid apology came out slurred. "I thought I was supposed to come after school; I didn't mean to interrupt."

"It's quite alright," replied the woman, who burst in a chuckle. "We were finishing up anyway. You just gave me quite the startle! Thank you Dean Foster, and I'll be sure to reach out to you again."

The woman presently left, and Phillip took her place in one of the comfortable chairs that sat across from the dean's desk.

"Teleport outside the office next time, please," requested Dean Foster. "You could have accidentally teleported into her, but good control overall. I see you're still teleporting onto the X."

"Of course," responded Phillip, sincerely. "It won't happen again."

"Now, let's get on with things. You said you were able to access the Archives a few weeks ago, and I'm sorry that I had brushed you aside that day. I haven't asked you anymore about it because I knew you were focused on the tournament. Have you returned since then?"

Phillip shook his head.

"Well, I'd like you to go again. It may help us get you back to your own time," explained the dean, who hesitated before continuing. "Do you think you can take me with you?"

Phillip furrowed his brow, thinking of Lucia and Septimus before declaring, "Yes. I think I can, but I haven't done it before. I know it's possible at least."

The dean reached out to grab his student's hand. Phillip braced himself, as he wasn't sure how an extra person would affect his ability to navigate. In a fraction of a split second, he teleported, and the two were surrounded by bookshelves. Phillip watched the dean look around in disappointment.

"This is just the school library," observed the dean, disappointed. "What happened?"

Phillip sighed, dismayed with himself for failing.

"Sorry, I think that I was thinking about the Archives, a grand portion of which is a sort of library. But I'm not supposed to. Can I try again?"

Once again, the dean lightly laid his hand on Phillip's shoulder, and Phillip himself cleared his mind. It took a while, but the dean was patient. Eventually, the air became stale, and a storm of silence overtook Phillip's senses. Since he was normally on autopilot, the young traveler had never noticed how... blank the Archives could be, but the juxtaposition to the typically tranquil school library made him realize how different this non-place was. When he opened his eyes, the endless maze of books, shelves, and marble floors confirmed that they had arrived. Dean Foster himself was left speechless, and Phillip followed his gaze upward.

"I don't think I ever noticed that," noted Phillip, seeing how there was no roof, just an endless space above him.

"How do you find out which books you want to read?" asked Dean Foster, but all Phillip could do was shrug. He himself was still new to the way that the Archives functioned.

"You have to spend some time exploring, but eventually you just figure it out," he guessed, based on what Lucia had told him.

From the corner of his eye, Phillip spotted the young Roman girl.

"Lucia? Why are you always present whenever I come?"

"Perhaps it is that you have somehow made an attachment to me. Septimus is never too far away whenever he arrives either. I am flattered that I mean that much to you. And you were able to bring a friend this time," she noted.

Dean Foster bowed and introduced himself, "Hello, I'm Reginald Foster. I am very happy to hear the voice of an ancient Latin speaker. It reminds me of my youth, when I studied the language."

Lucia's lips turned upwards in an amused smile, and she pursed them together as though she was trying to prevent herself from laughing.

"I see that you truly speak my language. However, the way you speak is not like a native Roman. Your words and cadence are... unbalanced."

The dean himself seemed flustered at what she meant, and Phillip himself didn't completely understand either. He had never studied Latin since his parents were adamant that he take Greek instead.

"If you were to speak in English, she would hear you in Latin," explained Phillip to his mentor. "In fact, I've been hearing this whole conversation in English."

"He is right," confirmed Lucia. "I met a man, Greek. If I wanted to, I could hear him in Greek, but I was also able to hear him in Latin if I chose to. You can learn to choose which language to converse in."

"I didn't know that," stated Phillip.

"There is much yet that you do not know. Now, I suppose I can help you find information on whatever subject you seem to be interested in. By the way, did you ever determine the state of your illusion?"

"Illusion?" echoed the dean. "Is this about your dream invasion?"

Lucia looked at the pair. She had not meant to give out information that was not hers to begin with, and she let Phillip explain for himself his situation

"Well, it's no secret that time-travel (to the past) has long been thought impossible. I had discussed with Lucia and Septimus the possibility that I was under an advanced enchantment or possession."

The dean could not help but sigh, "I suppose that's a reasonable consideration, and I understand why you didn't ask me about it. If I were a part of the illusion, I would have likely tried to lead you astray. I hope my presence here confirms that I am in fact real and corporeal."

"Unless you were the one behind it," retorted Lucia, not meaning to be rude. Phillip noticed that she had a soft yet blunt way about her. The ancients themselves were not caught up in the modern notions of politeness that Phillip had grown up with. In fact, he noticed at times that Dean Foster exhibited a sort of antiquated gruffness that was missing in contemporary life. Yet, Lucia continued, “I don’t think you are, though. At least not from my initial perception of your countenance.”

“I appreciate that,” scoffed the dean, who then turned to Phillip. “It only reminds me that I need to train you on psychological defenses. For now, I was hoping to find any sort of information on time travel.”

“I can help you with that, but it will take some time for us to actually find whatever sort of book, scrolls, or codex that you want. Follow me.”

The trio walked down the aisle of shelves, and Phillip took note of the wooden handiwork. The carpentry shone through both through the creaking floorboards and immaculately designed bookshelves. Patterns of leaves, Celtic interlace, and Greek key among others framed a variety of books that Phillip had never seen before.

“Wait a second!” shouted Phillip, who had not meant to be so loud.

“What is it?” asked the dean, startled.

Lucia herself turned to face Phillip, curious as to what he was about to say.

“You said that things here don’t decay or change. How come the floorboards are creaking then?”

He hadn’t meant to sound so accusing, but Lucia didn’t ever seem to take offense to anything.

Motioning towards the shelves, she answered, "Take another look at the material."

Phillip obliged and read various titles such as *A Map of Cedar Varieties*, *The Arboreal Atlas*, *The Hidden Life of Trees*, etc.

"They're all about trees and wood," noted Phillip.

Lucia nodded and continued to lead them before speaking.

"I thought I had explained this to you last time, but maybe I was not clear. The Archives don't just give you information through books. Knowledge and wisdom is not just read or looked at, but it is experienced. In a way, you must learn to read the Archives if you are ever going to be able to navigate through it. The creaks you hear are by design. The floorboards store the sound, the texture, even the taste of these planks of wood. If you were to take more than a moment's glance at the marble you saw when you first discovered the Archives, you would notice that it told the story of patterns, material, of its own creation."

As she walked, she picked up a loose part of ivory stola that began to drag on the ground. The revelation she had delivered might seem like old news to her, but even Dean Foster himself was eating up every word that came out of her mouth.

"You say that there's an experience of taste. Is there food here?" asked Phillip, imagining how wonderful it would be to eat and never gain weight.

"If there were, you wouldn't be able to consume it," she replied before coming to a stop. "Here we are."

She had led them to a desk with a bell on it not unlike the first one that Phillip had encountered.

"Don't ring the bell," he instructed the dean.

"I wasn't going to, but why not?"

"We do not do such a thing," answered Lucia, which did not seem to satisfy the dean's query. Nonetheless, he accepted the command with humility.

The young roman girl scurried around the desk and bent down to grab something from under it. When she arose, she presented them a cylindrical canister with a sliding door and a piece of paper as well as a thin piece of what looked like graphite.

"Don't worry, I always keep charcoal on me just in case I want to jot something down, and you should, too. It is very useful. Now, let me explain. We write down what we want to know and we put it in this glass container here. We close it, and the information written on it attracts information of a similar type. We use the container then as a type of lantern that shines us towards whatever we want to know. Do you understand?"

Phillip took a second to follow along, and the dean nodded with pure amazement on his face. It made Phillip himself wonder whether or not he himself was appreciating this resource as much as he should be - almost like a child on vacation faced with the ruins of an empire that he knows nothing about.

"What should we say?" asked Lucia, staring at the two for an answer. Phillip himself only looked at his teacher, trusting that he would be better able to put into words what they wanted to know.

"Time-travel. Teleportation," he stated.

"That cannot be it," countered Lucia. "Do you have any idea how many books, paintings, and the rest are in this place? Fiction and reality? You must be more specific. You must have intention behind the request."

The dean asked for the charcoal and began writing, while it dawned on Phillip just how vast the Archives were. No wonder his mind had shielded him from comprehending the enormity; the idea of infinity was useful in theory, but daunting as an experience. It didn't take long for the dean to finish up writing, and he handed the materials back to Lucia.

"I'll let you do the honors, as you are more familiar with it."

She examined his calligraphy for a second (which Phillip knew was beautiful beyond compare) before folding the sheet neatly and stuffing it into the cylinder. There was no incantation, no magic even. Phillip watched her turn the dial, waiting for the contraption to glow, vibrate, or display a map of some sort. None of the above happened. In fact, it seemed like nothing was happening at all, but Lucia nodded and motioned for them to follow her.

"There are a few different ones we could try, but through its own science, this will lead us to whatever source of knowledge will best for us," clarified Lucia.

As Phillip followed her, he noticed that the whole map of the Archives had changed. He had witnessed no graduation, no instance of reformation of his surroundings, yet he found himself in a completely different environment to the arboreal section he was previously in.

"If this place is infinite, Lucia, then how are you able to get to where we are going so quickly?" he questioned.

"There are places within places," she said. It frustrated him that she would say stuff that to her sounded obvious and detailed, but was wildly mysterious and esoteric from his point of view. It was not as though she meant it to be obscure; it was only that her enigmatic way of speech made his own shortcomings of knowledge abundantly clear.

"Hmm... I suppose there's some sort of mathematical way to group a set of information," postulated Dean Foster.

"I do not often meditate on those kinds of abstractions," was all Lucia had to say, as though she were trying to express modesty.

"You mean you stay in here all this time, but you don't bother to learn advanced mathematics?" said Phillip, a little too sharply. He was ashamed of himself, but was thankful that Lucia always received his words gracefully.

"I like geometry and patterns, but I suppose I do not have a leaning towards advanced physics. I like to read about philosophy, spirituality, and the natural world. That is why you found me in the aquarium last time. I was searching for the fish that swallowed Jonah."

"There's an aquarium?" asked Dean Foster excitedly. "This place is incredible. I understand why you stay here indefinitely."

"I take my refuge here because wicked people set out to kill me for being a Christian."

Dean Foster raised his eyebrows at that response, but didn't ask for any extrapolation of events. By that moment, Lucia declared that they had arrived and held out her hand, into which a book flew into it from the top shelf. It bolted out as fast as a missile, and for a second

Phillip was worried that it would hurt her. Lucia herself showed no sign of pain and only briefly looked at the cover before handing it to Dean Foster.

"*A Treatise on Movement in Time*," he read aloud. "Can we take this with us?"

"You cannot," she expressed, and Phillip suspected that she was tired of telling ill-informed magi the same thing.

"We have all the time in the world to read here, though," expounded Phillip. "I took ages to learn about the illusion magic, but I got to look at sea creatures when I got bored."

The dean sat down and sighed, "I'm too old for this. Is there a copy for my student to read with me?"

Lucia grabbed the copy in his hands, but when the dean let go, his book dropped. Lucia herself held a duplicate in her own hands, which she handed to Phillip. For herself, she retained a third copy and sat down next to them to read. Neither the dean nor Phillip had seen anything casting that physically duplicated an object before, but it made sense. Information here isn't physical, and they would all be able to grasp it simultaneously. Dean Foster himself picked up his dropped copy and began to read while Phillip sat down against the shelf to start with him. To his surprise, the hard floor he sat on and the disruptive shape of the bookshelf did not discomfort him. Nonetheless, the pages on the inside were confusing and boring, and he struggled to concentrate.

Lucia was the first to finish, which didn't surprise Phillip. If she had lodged in here for as long as she claimed (an indescribably amount of time), then her patience and reading comprehension was far beyond any of theirs. Phillip watched as she took out another book from the shelf and observed that the dean was already halfway through the book (a few hundred years of practice and a social-media free brain must be healthy). Dejected, Phillip began to read only the second chapter, only grasping fifty percent of what the words meant to convey. Hopefully, the dean or Lucia would be able to help him with the material. By the end of the fifth chapter, Phillip had given up and began tracing his fingers along the markings of the marble floor he sat on. After what seemed like a century, the dean was finishing up, and Lucia was halfway through her third book.

"Well, that was interesting, informative, and at the same time rather useless, wouldn't you say Lucia?"

He hadn't bothered to address Phillip, realizing that the subject matter was probably far beyond his level. Lucia herself shrugged (*a modern American gesture*, considered Phillip, wondering if body language was likewise translated.

"It's out of our hands," she answered. "Phillip will need to find his way home through the Archives by himself."

"Well, there you have it. The best I can do is train you. Shall we go back?"

Phillip rolled his eyes in exasperation.

"I'm tired of not understanding any of this stuff," he sighed.

Although he considered leaving Dean Foster behind in resentment, he hurriedly grabbed onto him and teleported them back to 1969. At this point, he was mentally exasperated, frustrated, and ultimately, demoralized. His mood had soured to the point of rudeness, ignoring Lucia completely when he left.

Seeing his attitude, the dean said to Phillip, "I understand that we didn't find the answers you want, but I don't want you to give up hope. You have friends here now, and things aren't so bad, are they?"

"That's just another problem," replied Phillip. "I'm going to miss being here, at this point in time, as much as I currently miss my family and friends. Every day that I'm here strengthens my yoke to this year. I'm worried that I'll never be able to go back. I'm worried that things will change to the point that there's nothing for me to go back to."

Dean Foster nodded in understanding, but Phillip could see that he was struggling to formulate words that would provide comfort and assistance. Eventually, he held out his firm and hardened hand, saying, "Whether or not you will like the consequences, you must act. I'm here to help you as much as I can, but even I am not infallible. Come, let's return."

II

A SOBERING SOJOURN

Classes had helped Phillip to recover his mood, but once again, he had Cardinal Key to himself. Over the summer, he got to know Dean Foster very well, but spending Thanksgiving week alone was different. Again, he grappled with the depression that often followed solitude. If he had been at home, his family would probably have started the Advent fast already, and he would have been talking to Mark on the phone almost every day.

"You're a traveler," advised Dean Foster while the two were seated at dinner. "You can go literally anywhere in the world! Do you know how many people would kill to have your aptitude? Literally! Isn't there anywhere you want to see?"

Phillip stared at his cottage pie for a second, struggling to come up with an answer.

"I'm not sure. I'll have to think about it."

Dean Foster returned to reading his newspaper while Phillip considered where he might want to travel to. Half the world was out of the question - his father told him about how it wasn't even safe for magi under the communist regimes in Eastern Europe. However, he did want to have an Orthodox experience, and another thought came to him.

"I think I'm going to go to California tomorrow. To a place called Platina."

"Alright," said Dean Foster without looking up. He was clearly absorbed in whatever news was going on, and Platina didn't have much of a meaning for anyone anywhere yet.

Phillip didn't bother to wake up early the next morning as California was three hours behind. He did, however, have to go to the library to look for a map so that he could plan out his trip. Although Phillip found the small community after a long time of looking, he couldn't figure out where the monastery would be. There didn't seem to be any towns nearby either. After an hour of searching, Phillip gave up. He would just teleport to Route 36 and hope for the best. At the end of the day, he could always teleport back to Cardinal Key.

In an instant, Phillip was surrounded by the California wilderness, divided into two parts by the state highway. He took a second to stare at the road sign and admire how accurate his teleportation had become before heading down the street. True to the impatience of his generation, Phillip soon took to teleporting moderate sized distances in order to more quickly survey the area. Although he enjoyed hiking and nature as much as anyone else (he did trek into an Enchanted Forest after all), he was on a mission.

He had been teleporting randomly for what felt like hours when eventually, he came across a small neighborhood nestled in the mountains. Phillip wasn't sure if anyone here knew about the monastery that he was looking for, but it couldn't hurt to ask. Spotting a small, rundown store that seemed to double as the owner's home, Phillip entered. If anyone here knew about the community, it would certainly be the shopkeeper.

The bell chimed when Phillip opened the door, summoning the lonely shopkeeper to greet him. Unlike Virginia, the atmosphere here was dry and the store itself was stale. Apart from asking for directions, Phillip needed to buy refreshment.

"Hello," greeted the shopkeeper. "How can I help you today?"

"Yes, do you sell any beverages?"

The older woman, tanned from her time in the west coast sun, motioned for Phillip to follow her to the refrigerated section.

"You're not from around here are you. Passing through?"

"Yes," replied Phillip. "As a matter of fact, I was hoping you could tell me if you knew which way the monastery was."

"Oh, the new one? I think it opened about a year ago, but I've met a couple of young folk from there already. I can show you on the map if you'd like."

Phillip smiled gratefully, knowing that that was the best case scenario he could hope for. He pulled out a cold glass coke and purchased it along with a map of the area. The shopkeeper was kind enough to give a detailed account of where the monastery would be, and Phillip studied the map intensely as she rang up the sale. After paying, Phillip found a secluded spot nearby. Before he could teleport again, he would have to take a large swig of coke to recharge.

His magic felt slower this time, but that was to be expected after several hours of traveling in the California heat. His precision was also off, but he was still able to land several yards away from the monastery, on a dirt road that looked horrendous to drive over. Phillip took a few steps forward, but hesitated. He had no idea how to explain who he was or how he got there or why he was even there in the first place. However, he had already spent so much time trying to find the place, he didn't know what to do. Moreover, he wasn't sure if they were taking visitors yet, nor did he know how they would react to magi. It was still a contentious topic in the Christian community. After several minutes of staring at the quiet building, he decided to go back to Cardinal Key, ashamed of his own cowardice.

***

The scent of fisherman's pie was warm and welcoming in the colder weather. Having nothing else to do, Phillip had taken to making dinner for him and the dean, who himself was grateful. Over the summer, Phillip explained to him the Orthodox rule of fasting and was surprised at the dean's kind taking to it. According to him, it had reminded him of his youth when giving up meat was a regular occurrence among the faithful. In fact, there had once been a law in England which enforced fasting, the remnants of which had finally been repealed this very year.

The two now sat down at a small circular table in the dean's personal cottage. Nights like these were good opportunities for Phillip to practice his table manners, though the dean never said anything to him about any faux pas. In fact, he wished the dean was more talkative, but most nights, he just read his newspaper. Seeing Phillip's downcast look, though, the dean decided to converse.

"How was your adventure today?" he asked.

"'Twas for naught," replied Phillip, who found himself unintentionally mimicking the dean's linguistic anachronisms from time to time.

"What happened?" pursued the dean.

"I guess I got cold feet," answered Phillip. When he saw the dean waiting for an explanation, he continued. "You see, there's a new monastery that will become famous, and there's a monk that's going to become famous. I'll spare you the future details since I know you don't like it, but I thought I would go see it. I spent a lot of time looking for it, but when I got there, I realized how silly I was being. I can't just show up there out of the blue without explaining how I got there or why I was there. It's like I was just trespassing. I feel like a spineless coward."

The dean sat for a long moment while thinking.

"No, I don't think so," he finally said. "I don't know much about monasteries as I've only been to a couple on the continent. By the time I had been born, they were all dissolved. However, I can lament the fact that things are so different than they used to be. Nowadays, everything is about '*me, me, me*,' and you see it especially among this current generation of youth. Everything is atomized to the individual - his rights, his property, his own business. 'Twas not so long ago when one could go to his neighbor's house in the evening and ask for a match or for some sugar. People cared about each other. There was a community. To an extent, there still is, but I see it falling apart, and it is nowhere near as strong as it was a few centuries ago. I can only imagine how much worse it will become in the future, Phillip. Dinner tonight is delicious by the way. Your cooking is getting better and better. You're not using magic to make it, are you?"

12

FIGHT AND FLIGHT

The rest of the year was finishing up smoothly, and the atmosphere in the Elementafl club had calmed down. At this point, they had only met to play cordial games with each other, letting off some steam while they were studying for their pre-holiday exams. Betty and Phillip themselves had set aside their board in order to put their heads together for their upcoming physics project. They had already successfully constructed a pulley that used magic to lift up a small box without any counterweight (in essence, a simplified Leverate). Now, they just had to double check their calculations and prepare for their presentation.

Sally and Glenn were the next to come in, and Betty had commented how she had been seeing the two spend more time together recently. Phillip smirked, but desperately needed to focus on meteorology, his most challenging subject.

"If Nicholas weren't so jealous, I'd ask him to help me," commented Phillip.

"He probably won't even show up tonight. He always gets so stressed about his grades," responded Betty. "Not that I'm any better. I'm anxious about my performance in class, too."

"Isn't that the truth," agreed Glenn from their left. He and Sally were going back and forth in Elementafl, but he explained that they both were struggling in Latin. "I feel like I never have enough time to study everything that I want to. Does your aptitude work with only space or can manipulate time as well, Phillip? Like a chronologist."

Glenn's rapid yet coherent train of thought had caught Phillip off guard, especially considering the proximity Glenn's question had towards Phillip's secret. Before he could respond, Sally interjected.

"Don't be ridiculous, Glenn. Everybody knows that time-travel is impossible. That stuff only happens in H.G. Wells, right?"

"Yes," lied Phillip, who was growing tired of having to do so. "However, there is a place I can go to. It's called the Archives, and time doesn't really function there normally. It has all sorts of information, and you could study for however long you want to in preparation for your exams."

"Would you be able to take us there?" asked Betty, a blonde strand falling in front of her ice-blue eyes. It struck Phillip how similar the shade was to his sister's, and he didn't think that he would be able to deny her.

"Well, sure. I can take all of you if you want. You'll need to hold on to me," he instructed.

He hadn't explained the process too well, and they each individually grabbed onto him. Glenn kept an iron grip on his wrist, which made it difficult for him to clear his mind at first. Nonetheless, with experience came ease, and this time, Phillip had no problem delivering his four peers to the endless expanse of knowledge that existed outside time and space.

"Wow!" exclaimed Sally. "I could get lost here!"

"It is not only possible but likely if you are not careful," replied Lucia, who was sitting criss-crossed and charcoal in hand. From the looks of it, she had taken up studying abstract algebra since her last meeting with Phillip, likely overtaking the dean in his knowledge at this point. "I see you have brought new friends this time. Welcome."

It was strange for Phillip hearing her speak like this. It was not typical of her to sound facetious, as though she had not really meant what she was saying. Perhaps Phillip had gone too far this time by bringing so many people - kids - to the Archives, yet he did not feel as though Lucia would chastise him publicly.

"Yes," answered Phillip, a little nervous. "Everyone, this is Lucia. She's a bona fide Roman. Like I said, time doesn't really pass here, so there are all sorts of folk who come through. By the way, Lucia, have you seen Septimus recently? I was hoping to talk to him about my... thing."

He had wanted to keep his time-traveling abilities private, especially since he had just lied about it to his friends. Lucia, however, had no such qualms about that, likely not seeing any reason to keep it a secret.

"Oh the time-travel conundrum? It is true; he is around here somewhere," she replied.

"You *just* said time-travel was impossible," noted Betty, but then the older Roman gentleman approached them.

"Phillip! I knew I would see you again this time. And you have learned to bring friends along with you. Each time I see you, you learn a new trick to our aptitude. Lucia has already given me the rundown, and I had recently collected a scroll. I am going now to find it."

Phillip was heartened that Septimus had not taken to the group with a negative undertone, and he was even more pleased at the possibility of a final solution to his unwarranted journey. He looked around at the friends he had made, all to a degree taken to their surroundings, and had to admit that he was sorry to be departing from them. Betty herself stood by him, yet he was unsure of what to say.

"So are you trying to time travel or you are a time-traveler?" she posed, but before Phillip answered her question she continued. "I guess that would explain a lot. I feel I should be upset at you for keeping it hidden, but I suppose I understand why you had to. I'll miss you when you go back to your time."

It was as heart-warming of a good-bye that he was ever going to get, but before he could respond in turn, Septimus had begun to come back, accompanied by a young girl who looked almost like Lucia. Except it couldn't be her because she had sat back down and continued with her study of advanced mathematics. Besides, this girl was dressed in modern clothes.

"Phillip!" she shouted, and for a moment he stood still, awestruck. It simply was not possible.

"Kalina?" he exclaimed in turn, though it turned out to be more of a question of disbelief. Yet, there was no other way to explain it, and in his excitement he rushed to embrace his younger sister. "You're taller than I remembered."

"You look older," she said in turn.

Just then, a creeping feeling of darkness had overcome the reunited siblings, and shadowy cloaked figures began to sulk throughout the bookshelves. One tall, prominent woman drew the attention into herself, causing Lucia to leap to her feet.

"You!" she yelled out, pointing at the grand, olive skinned woman.

At this point, her minions had surrounded them, and for the first time Phillip had noticed that Kalina had brought with her friends as well, recognizing Aisling and Robert. They appeared not to be worried, but his own entourage seemed to cower. Lucia herself held a defiant look. Obviously she recognized the woman, and Phillip couldn't imagine what kind of person it would take to stir such a fire upon the gentle damsel he had come to know. After a moment of consideration, Phillip began to connect her appearance to that of the aerial woman who had invaded his dream: Diana.

PART 2:
INTERMISSIONS

THE MISTRESS

"Did you get it?"

"Yes, though I would like to know what you're planning on doing with only a tiny drop of traveler's blood."

"You always were so circular in your thinking, Carannog. No vision, no purpose, no progress. Just an asteroid trapped in orbit."

Cara didn't bother to react or respond to Dido; she knew her dig was meant as a test and never gave it anymore thought. She watched Dido take the Elementafl piece, where Cara had cleverly hid a prick in order to collect the mysterious student's blood. It was really quite simple, and the girl she targeted was rather easy to possess. The hardest part was toying with Elementafl board. She couldn't win too easily, but had to draw the game out. Forcing the boy to lose by making him run out of time was the best option. Her student still won and there was no suspicious activity to point back to her.

Dido, or Diana as she liked to be called by her servants, unscrewed the top, pulling out the hidden vial that stored the sanguine essence before pouring it into a petri dish. Her senior always had a liking for mixing modern science with magic; it felt profane. Some people thought that magic and science were the same thing; others thought they were opposed. Cara herself tended to be biased towards the latter, where magic and witchcraft worked together to allow those chosen few to mold the world into their own image. That is how it was in the old days, when magic wasn't dissected and studied, but was manipulated by a selected caste.

If she had to guess what her ancient mentor was up to, she would support the hypothesis of creating some sort of golem. It would explain the petri dish, the Hebrew letters, and runes older than Carannog herself (which said a lot since she was almost two thousand years old). Whatever Dido's plans were, Cara was clearly not involved - at least not yet. No matter - Cara was used to doing her own private scheming for at least a millennium. In a few moments, she would be dismissed and would go back to her New World playground.

THE WITCH

"Hello, ma'am. How can I help you today?"

"I'm here for a walk-in appointment with Detective Albert Christie."

"I'm sorry, ma'am, but he doesn't do walk-in appointments. Can I leave a message for him?"

"Yes."

"Alright, may I see your ID please?"

The secretary looked at the driver's license and punched some numbers into her desktop phone before picking it up.

"Hello, there's a woman here saying she urgently needs to speak to Al. Her name is..." the secretary paused to double-check the ID. "Caroline Dalton."

Immediately, an alarm screeched and scarlet lights chaotically flashed all over the lobby. In a matter of seconds, several guards armed with semi-automatic rifles flooded the lobby, surrounding the nonchalant witch.

"Don't move! Put your hands above your head!" shouted one of them.

Despite the fact that the young secretary was cowering behind her desk, Cara could smell the sweet aroma of her fear. One of the guards approached her and placed her hands in iron cuffs. Of course, she didn't bother fighting back; that wasn't part of her plan. She wasn't afraid of being outmatched, either, but inwardly mocked the pathetic excuses of magi that detained her. The cuffs were downright ridiculous and she was embarrassed on their behalf. *Back in my day,* savages *knew how to forge iron that could really stop a witch from casting. They even knew how to trap fae. These degenerated monkeys know nothing - half of them probably have never even tried to achieve anything higher than basic magic.*

She decided to keep these thoughts to herself as she was led into an elevator to the bottom floor, where there were rows and rows of cells holding all sorts of prisoners. She caught a glimpse of a bushy-haired woman with skin as dark as ebony banging on the door. Her voice was muffled, but all it took was once glance for Cara to tell that she wasn't a real magus.

"What did this normie do? Light a candle?" she asked sarcastically. Cara, having lived for two millennia, considered the ban on pyromancy to be cowardly and incredibly neutering. *What do these idiots think was the catalyst for civilization?*

"Mind your own business," demanded the guard curtly. He came to a halt before a cell unlike the others. After opening the door he motioned her in. Before he could close it, she turned around and handed him a rusty pair of iron handcuffs.

"I don't think I'll be needing these anymore. Do you think you could hold on to them?"

The guard was startled for a moment, but that was all Cara needed to take control over him. She remembered one of her first lessons from her youth: *the loss of your own self-control is the beginning of another's power over you.*

"Better yet," she added, pressing a finger over his heart. "Why don't you take me to Detective Christie yourself? An elderly woman shouldn't have to wait too long in a dark, mangy cell."

(Of course, a few months ago, she had kept a young girl locked in a dark, dusty room for her own benefit.)

"That... makes... sense..." acquiesced the guard.

Cara admired his will to fight off her influence, but even in her weakened state, she could have outmatched five of him. *They don't make them like they used to*, she lamented. *Except for that quarterback. He could put up one hell of a fight even in a coma.* Cara both respected and resented Robert Nelson. On the one hand, she was proud that such strong druidry remained in her kinfolk, but on the other hand, she blamed him for consuming too much of her energy. *If it hadn't been for his drain on me, I would have been strong enough to overcome and consume Kalina's aptitude.*

By the time she had finished her thoughts, the guard was pressing the button on the elevator to the top floor. There were fortunately no other guards, but it wouldn't have mattered anyways. As they ascended the elevator, Cara casually inspected the myriad of safety runes and wards ethereally embedded into the building. They made the ones at Cardinal Kep look like cave-paintings. Still, Cara was disappointed in herself for not recognizing many of them. Naturally, she could decipher most of the magic, but there were modern sorts that she had never encountered before. *Maybe Dido is right. Maybe I do need to evolve. I'll show her.*

Finally, the elevator came to a stop with a ding and opened up to reveal an empty office space. *They must have known I was coming, so they cleared out.* Secretly, Cara was proud of herself for instilling such fear into professionally trained magi.

"Detective Christie's office is straight down and to the right," said the guard.

"Thank you. Now go."

The guard left while Cara slowly strode down the hall, merely perusing the empty cubicles with disinterest. Once she reached the end, she peered to her right. An open door was inviting her, and beyond it was the man she meant to meet. He didn't even so much as look up at her when she walked into his office, but he continued to type rapidly on his desktop. At first, she thought he hadn't noticed her, but he motioned her to sit down with one hand.

"I'll be with you in just a moment. I just need to fill this paperwork out real quickly. I'm sure you understand."

Cara didn't, but she obliged anyway. It didn't take long for Detective Christie to shut off his monitor and turn his attention to her.

"Why are you here, Ms. Dalton?"

"Well, I'm here to help you."

Ms. Dalton stared intensely into his eyes, waiting for him to respond. However, he moved with such precision. Every one of his expressions was deliberate. It was almost like he was a robot. Surely everyone (almost everyone) had some sort of compelling habit or tic (with the exception of Dido). A fidgety finger, a shaky leg, a nervous laugh. Yet, Detective Christie didn't allow one hair to be out of shape. His glossy, gray eyes maintained a perfect equilibrium of constriction and dilation. *He's trying to prove something to me*, thought Cara. However, another look told her that he was trying to do what she had done to the guard. It was almost cute of him to think that he was at her level.

After a stiff silence that was more awkward than dramatic, Detective Christie mechanically shifted in his chair and asked, "How so? We already know about the girls, your little group of friends, and that you were kicked out."

Obviously true; information from Robert or Kalina; lucky guess as to why I'm here. Bluffing isn't going to get him too far.

"You hardly know anything. You don't know their names or what their real mission is. However, if you don't think I have any worthwhile information, I'll be on my way."

There was no immediate reaction or pleading. There was no quick movement or impulse to stop her. There was only the cool voice of the detective saying, "Naturally, your information would be valuable to our investigation. It seems that we may mutually benefit from a temporary partnership."

Success, thought Cara, pleased with herself. *I will have my revenge.*

PART 3: THE VISIONARY

13
TOKEN AND UNBROKEN

Kalina's eyes snapped open, focusing on the ambient sapphire light of her bedroom. Her heart still raced as she reached for her token, a small two-by-two Rubik's Cube that she kept with her at all times. As she solved the easy puzzle, her breath returned to normal, and her body relaxed. She could be sure now that she was still awake. Since the beginning of the summer, she had been tiptoeing into higher planes of existence. Without any formal training, she often found the line between the physical and psychic realms to become blurred. Even more frightening, she often found herself unsure whether or not she was in her body, her mind, or merely a dream (nightmare, more likely). After learning about tokens in a movie, she decided to get one. It had to be a puzzle - nothing too hard to solve, but tricky enough to be a challenge in a dream. The Rubik's Cube was perfect for her since she knew that she wouldn't be able to keep track of the colors in a mere dream.

Tonight's terror trap had been especially jarring; however, she should have known it to be nothing more. Like her vision a few months ago, she had seen Dalton reaching towards her with her clawlike hands. In the nightmare, Kalina found herself unable to move - trapped in a cocoon of ice - similar to the feeling of paralysis she experienced when Dalton had kidnapped her last year. Just as Kalina was about to break free, Dalton had set her on fire, and that's when everything went black, startling Kalina out of her nightmare.

With her adrenaline still keeping her awake, Kalina decided to move on to the three-by-three Rubik's Cube that she kept on her nightstand. It wasn't small enough to keep with her at all times, but she did find it relaxing. She checked her phone and sighed, she would have to wake up in a couple of hours since she and her mom would be driving to Cardinal Key early. *No matter, I'll sleep in the car if I can or when I get there.* She wasn't even sure if she would be able to fall back asleep, so she decided to solve the four-by-four a few times, and then the five-by-five.

***

The car had been atypically silent as Kalina and her mother drove to Cardinal Key Academy. Come to think of it, the whole house had felt immobile since Phillip's disappearance. Kalina was tempted to turn on the radio or listen to music on her headphones, but having some quiet company appealed to her. Eventually, her mother began to converse.

"Sister Maryam has been asking about you, by the way."

"Oh," replied Kalina, who hadn't visited to the convent in a while. The nun's warning about her aptitude echoed in her head, but she was confident that she could now capably handle her visions. "Can you say 'hi' to her for me please?"

"Of course," replied Catherine Todorova, almost a little too briefly.

"I have Maura as a roommate again this year," continued Kalina, welcoming the friendly change in atmosphere. It had only been her and her mother after all since her father decided to stay home.

"Oh, that's wonderful. What about Laurelle? Is she with you?"

"No, she was paired with Alice, but I think they're friends. They both play earth in stoickee so that might be how they got matched."

"That's nice."

Last year, Kalina would have expected her parents - her mother especially - to be nosier about her academics and social life, but now that Phillip was gone, everything was different. Her father had been completely silent most dinners, and her mother spent her days fervently in prayer when she wasn't at church services or doing chores. Kalina herself had been feeling horrible because she didn't feel the same way that they did. She couldn't mourn the loss of Phillip because she knew that he was safe - or will be - or was. She had tried to tell her own parents that Phillip was fine, but if they did believe her (which she doubted), it didn't change anything. He was gone - end of story.

Her parents didn't even ask Kalina about her aptitude test, which to be completely honest, had upset her a little bit. All the same, the slip of paper she was given a week after her the strange trial had only one word written on it: *visionary*. *What does that even mean?* Kalina asked herself. She had always thought of herself as a clairvoyant, an oracle, even some sort of sibyl... but a "visionary?" Was that really the vocabulary they chose to describe someone with her gifts? A visionary was someone like Steve Jobs or Elon Musk, not her. *I'm much more powerful than some rich technocrat. Dr. Toumi and Dean Schulz should have recognized that when they had fallen to their knees.* That being said, Robert did tell her that that kind of stuff happened all the time to them, but he refused to go into detail about his own aptitude test - or others, which was a respectable commitment to privacy. *There's been a big push to systematize magical terminology,* he had explained to her. *That's why we say things like geokinesis instead of geomancy now. There was much confusion and competition between magi, witches, kings, priests, etc. in the past, but since AIMM, it's been much easier to scientize the field. The only exception being psychic magic, which has proven difficult to study in an empirical method. That's why the term "intellectual" magic hasn't quite caught on yet.*

After a further, silent drive (Kalina's mom only rarely listened to secular music now), the dense woods opened up to reveal the grounds of Cardinal Key Academy. Unlike last year, Kalina was greeted by a quieter campus as her mother decided to take her early on Saturday morning to drop her off. The only other time she had seen the school grounds this empty was when she had reappeared out of the Enchanted Forest forty days after she was kidnapped by her former teacher and mentor. To her, only one day had passed, but when she had come back, she had discovered that everybody else was on spring break and her brother was nowhere to be found. Catherine Todorova parked the car as normal, and Kalina got out to open the trunk. Her mother took more time to get out to say goodbye to her daughter.

"Do you want me to come inside with you?" she asked.

Kalina hesitated before she answered, "No, I think I'm okay... but you can if you want to."

"No, that's fine, I'm just going to head home so that I can prepare dinner for your father."

"Alright, well goodbye, then," said Kalina, giving her mother a hug and a kiss before turning around to head to her dorm. As a seventh grader, she got to be on the sixth floor this time, and as she already knew, Maura would be her roommate.

***

"KALINA!" squealed a shrill voice.

Of course Kalina had heard her first and immediately jumped up from her bed to greet Maura, whose ginger hair bounced along as she likewise rushed to meet her friend. They embraced each other in a hug before catching up.

"Maura! Did you just get here?" greeted Kalina. "Oh, hi, Mrs. Donovan."

"Hi Kalina. Is your mom here?" asked Maura's mom, who Kalina thought was a little intimidating.

"No, she left already. We got here earlier this morning."

"Well, say 'hello' to her for me please. Now that I've got Maura settled, I'm going to help Aisling. Maura, why don't you meet with me and your sister in fifteen minutes so we can all say goodbye together."

"Okay, mom."

It was barely a half-second, but Kalina thought she might have seen an unpleasant gulp or hint of discomfort. *No, maybe not. Maybe I'm just making up microexpressions in my head.* She double checked her pocket for her Rubik's Cube, and the touch of it was strong enough to bring Kalina back to earth. As soon as her mother left the dorm, Maura pivoted on one heel towards Kalina.

"I have so much to tell you," she said in a low, conspiratorial tone.

"Really?" prompted Kalina, as she helped Maura unpack her belongings.

"You'll never guess what happened over the summer," squeaked Maura.

"Aisling formally broke up with Robert and started officially dating Mark?" guessed Kalina, who already knew about the situation from talking to Robert.

"Um... actually, yeah, exactly that. I forgot that you have this uncanny intuition - even though you refuse to tell us your aptitude."

Kalina could have corrected her, but she liked basking in her own aura of mystique. Maura squinted her eyes, as though she were trying to telepathically pry information out of Kalina's head. She wasn't worried, though, as she knew that Maura had a physical aptitude as an acoustician. Still, Maura did have street smarts and was known to be fairly adept at reading people.

"Anyways," continued Kalina. "What do your parents think of the relationship?"

"They're fine with it."

A lie, perceived Kalina. *There's something wrong at home. I knew it. I just don't know what exactly is happening.* Before Kalina could steer the conversation from that direction, Maura steered the conversation to a different topic.

"By the way, have you heard from Laurelle at all? I tried reaching out to her, but she hasn't responded."

"No, she was pretty angry that she didn't test for an aptitude."

"Did she tell you that? She was acting like she was fine with it. Plus, her parents didn't seem upset. I mean, they are both only half-magi, so maybe that has something to do with it..."

"She was *livid*," asserted Kalina, who marveled that Maura couldn't see past Laurelle's facade of nonchalance." But of course her parents were fine with it. I think her father has an aptitude, but her mother doesn't."

"Hmm... are you sure you're *not* an empath?" teased Maura, who seemed to know that Kalina's aptitude was psychic in nature.

DING

Although both Kalina and Maura instinctively reached for their phones, only Maura had something to say.

"It's my mom. She's about to head out. Want to go down so we can go to closets together?"

"I've been waiting for you to ask!"

The two headed down, talking about how they were going to prepare for the semester ahead of them. Now that they were in seventh grade, they had a lot more freedom and were more comfortable with being at school by themselves. They were still middle-schoolers, but they were ready to take on the entire campus.

14
THE SLOW START

Tiny black shapes stared up at Kalina, who was trying to make sense of them. She closed her eyes for a second and reopened them. *Why did they give us so much homework after the first week?*

"My brain is dead," declared Kalina to Maura. "Do you want to go get some fuel?"

"Ach, I thought you would never bring it up. I've reread this paragraph like five times already. I feel like we should have learned all this last year!"

Maura violently snapped her books shut and followed Kalina out the door. Their class as a whole had to have their entire curriculum readjusted since it turned out they were taught by a witch the previous year. Unlike most seventh graders, they *all* had to take a diagnostic test on their first day to check what they've learned and what they still need to be educated or re-educated on.

As the pair of roommates walked down the hall, Alice, who didn't so much as look up at them, passed by. Her footsteps sounded heavy as she marched down to Stephanie's dorm and rapped on the door.

"It's only the first week. What do you think is going on with her?" asked Maura.

"I was just about to ask you the same."

"No idea," replied Maura. "We're supposed to play field hockey one-on-one tomorrow though, so maybe I'll ask her then."

Kalina sighed and opened the door to the stairway, and Maura played with the acoustics of their echoing footsteps. Kalina didn't like it when her peers used magic uselessly, but she decided to keep her opinions to herself. It's not like anyone would listen to her, and the debate would only serve to cause contention. When they got to the lobby, Kalina was disappointed to see Mrs. Donna seated at the front desk. She knew that she would have to talk about her mom, and she was hoping it wouldn't be awkward.

"Where are you girls headed off to?" she asked. Mrs. Donna didn't mean to be nosey of course, and she could see where they were going in the log anyways. *She's just being friendly*, Kalina reminded herself.

"We're headed to the mess hall for dinner," answered Maura, as she penned her name in the checkout sheet for their grade.

"Oh, I heard they were having rotisserie chicken tonight! How's your mom been, Kalina? I haven't heard from her since - in a while. I'd like to catch up with her."

Mrs. Donna's slip-up wasn't lost on Kalina, who was worried that she would have to deal with everyone tiptoeing around the subject of Phillip for the whole year - or at least until she found him.

"She's managing," fibbed Kalina. "She's been keeping herself occupied with church activities."

That last part was definitely true, and as far as coping methods go, Kalina could think of worse ways to deal with a missing child. At least her mother was doing *something*. She felt as though her father just took it on the chin - as if Phillip's disappearance wasn't all that important, and the fact that the world kept spinning was simply enough for him. Maybe he believed Kalina when she said that Phillip was alive and that he would come back eventually. If so, why wasn't he acting normal? Once the two girls left the building, Kalina took a deep breath and sighed. *That wasn't so bad, and at least I've gotten that first interaction out of the way.*

"Are you alright, you've been sighing a lot," said Maura, with a face of concern that could match any worried mother's.

"Yeah, it's just the whole thing with Phillip, you know? And Mrs. Donna is friends with my mom, who *is* handling herself, I guess."

"I thought you said Phillip was alright and that you believed he time-traveled."

"He is, but I can't *prove* it, especially given that everyone thinks that time-travel is an impossibility. It doesn't change the fact that he's gone, either."

Maura shook her head. "I thought Aisling would have buried herself into her research over the summer, but she's nonstop been talking to Mark. I think something happened to them in the forest that they aren't telling anyone about - not even the detectives."

Kalina tried to recall the event of her kidnapping and escape, but her memory was fuzzy. All summer she had tried to find Phillip's mind somewhere in the aerial realm, but maybe she should have started from the beginning and made sense of the sequence of events from there.

"I don't want to think about that right now," scoffed Kalina. She didn't mean to make Maura feel awkward, but when she looked over to her friend, she noticed Maura grinding her teeth and looking down. Kalina kicked a rock into the grass and began monologuing. "Look, I admit it was scary, but it really wasn't that bad. I'm tired of everyone acting like I'm a fragile doll! I even have to waste my Saturday morning to see Dr. Toumi for an 'emotional evaluation!'"

"I hope you're not trash-talking my mentor."

Both Kalina and Maura jumped at the sudden appearance of Robert Nelson, who joined them on the path to the mess hall.

"Sorry to startle you. It's a new trick I learned - increasing others' blind spots. It's not technically illusion magic in case you're wondering."

He looked directly at Maura, who hid her red face. Kalina knew that he didn't always mean to read people's minds, but after Ms. Dalton put him into that coma last year, she could tell that something was different about his abilities. Even after just a few months since she last saw Robert, it was like his abilities were... open - like an overflowing water faucet. It was unnatural for him to bounce back as quickly as he did, even if he were as powerful as people say he is.

"Nice," was all Kalina could think of saying, and she was a little upset that she hadn't caught on to the subtle manipulation. "Do you want to join us? We're about to have dinner?"

"No thanks. I'm meeting up with the football team for dinner."

With that, Robert graciously opened the wooden doors for the two girls and they each headed inside to be greeted by a multitude of savory smells. Ms. Donna was right, and the aroma of lemon-herbed rotisserie chicken permeated the building. Friday was supposed to be a fasting day, but Kalina simply couldn't help herself. By the end of the night, she had feasted on two chicken quarters, a mountain of mashed potatoes, and several crispy roasted brussel sprouts. Not bad for a back-to-school dinner.

15

SESSIONS AND SUSPICIONS

The bright rays of sunlight slid through Kalina's blinds, shining their way directly on top of her eyelids. The uncomfortable heat of the morning light forced her to wake up, and she immediately checked her clock to make sure that she would have enough time to get ready for her session with Dr. Toumi. Right enough, her alarm would have gone off in another eight minutes, she hopped out of bed and began her morning routine. She wasn't totally sure what to expect from the trained psychologist and doctor. It wasn't likely that he would use his aptitude to pry too deeply into her, but she was disconcerted nonetheless. Robert's psychic abilities were easy to block for her, but that was for a multitude of reasons. He wasn't prying; she was used to his presence; he was recovering from a coma, and all the same, he was still just a student. In fact, if Robert's path was any indication of her own, it was more than likely that Dr. Toumi was going to offer her a mentorship.

The medical wing was always open when there were students on campus, and it was staffed not just by Dr. Toumi, but by three other nurses as well, one of whom she knew to be Stephanie's own mentor. Kalina made her way to Dr. Toumi's office, and although the door was ajar, she knocked to make her presence known.

"Good morning!" he greeted, cheerfully. "Please, come in, and close the door behind you.

"Good morning," replied Kalina, unsure where to begin.

"Yes, so I've spoken with your parents and Dean Schulz about having sessions with you based on your aptitude test and last year's incident."

"The kidnapping," clarified Kalina, bluntly.

"Yes... the kidnapping. I know that you talked with the investigators and your parents about it no doubt, but as the school's counselor it is my job that you are doing well physically, emotionally, and academically."

Clever, thought Kalina, *he sandwiched the 'emotional' part in there to not make me feel targeted. I'm still here, though, and no one else is - Aisling, Mark, and Robert were also a part of this, but I suppose being an older student has perks.*

"I see that you are suspicious. I can understand that based on what you've been through, having been betrayed by your former... 'mentor.'"

The way he stressed the word *mentor* bothered her for some reason. Kalina glared at him.

"I don't like being read like that," she said, and it was true. She had always been a private person.

"I'm sorry, I don't mean to pry, but even without my abilities your reaction was easy to read."

In response, Kalina put on the best poker face that she could manage. "What about now?"

"Ah, so you're testing me now?" chuckled Dr. Toumi. "I don't use my aptitude like that. I'm not like Robert; I don't read minds."

"How does your aptitude work then?" asked Kalina.

"Well, I can literally see people's emotional states. Not every empathic magus can do this, but I have synesthesia. For me, it looks like colors or shapes on people. Sometimes sounds."

"You can see auras?"

"They certainly look like auras, but they're more like atmospheres. It's like each person has their own weather pattern. This is actually something I have in common with Robert. When I was a kid, I used to get sensory overload from seeing the storm of emotions in other people."

"What do some of the emotions look like? Is sadness blue for example?" inquired Kalina, who was curious if the way his aptitude was visualized was similar to her own. To her, it was like strings being woven together or points of information traveling on a canvas.

"It's not like that. For me, sadness looks like a gray fog around someone. It's cold and wet, but we're not here to talk about me or my aptitude. I really need to make sure that you *are* doing well. I remember last year that you had some problems with socialization and maybe some depression."

Kalina was hoping to stall for a longer period of time. She disliked talking about herself too much, and she hated talking about her weaknesses. For now though, she would have to go along with the plan. There was no getting out of this, so she would just have to make the best out of a cumbersome situation. She could even benefit from it if she tried. Besides, Dr. Toumi was a genial man, and she doubted that he was secretly out to get her.

"Yeah, but I got over that eventually," answered Kalina. "My mother took me to visit a convent, and I got some advice from one of the nuns."

"Saint Nina's or Saint Ana's?" asked Dr. Toumi, reminding Kalina that he too was an Orthodox Christian. *Unlike Ms. Dalton*, she reflected spitefully.

"Saint Nina's. Have you been?"

"A couple times, actually. I'm sure you are aware that Dean Schulz and I worked over the summer to build an Orthodox chapel to go along with the Catholic and Protestant ones. We had to consult some experts on it."

"No, I didn't. Is Dean Schulz converting? That *would* explain the new beard."

Dr. Toumi chuckled at Kalina's remark before responding, "Yes, that *is* why he's growing a beard. I have to tell him that you said that."

Kalina awkwardly sat in her chair, unsure of why he thought that was so funny. She considered that it was a normal occurrence, and there *was* a stereotype associated with the catechumen beard.

"We're also working on setting up some philosophy courses, which as a precognizant, you would benefit greatly from. Moreover, since you have a powerful psychic aptitude, I'd like to offer my mentorship to you." Seeing Kalina hesitate, he added, "I've been able to help Robert control his aptitude, and I might be able to help you with yours."

He thinks that I'm hesitant to accept because of my past experience with Ms. Dalton, discerned Kalina. On the one hand, that was a strong reason why. However, the deeper reason was that Kalina wanted to explore the deeper parts of the psychic realm that she doubted he would let her near. She wanted to push herself to her true potential. *I need to push myself to my fullest potential. He'll just try to hold me back.*

"I'm sorry, Dr. Toumi. I'll come to the counseling sessions, but I think you know that my aptitude isn't mere cognition. There's something else that I've been warned not to share about with anyone."

Dr. Toumi sighed, "Yes I know, Dean Schulz and I worked over the results from your aptitude test for hours. I know we officially stated that you were a visionary, which is the modern and technical term. However, your aptitude closely aligns with the results for precognition, including some other abnormalities. That being said, you shouldn't have to figure out your aptitude on your own. You still need someone to help with your training. I'll talk to Dean Schulz about it."

"Thank you."

"Well, unless there's anything else you want to ask or share, I think this has been a pretty good starting session."

"Yes," replied Kalina. "I mean no, nothing else."

"Wonderful," he said, standing up to lead her out the door. "I trust you'll be attending the school's first Orthodox liturgy tomorrow? I expect many students to come out of curiosity, and we will need people to help with the chanting. A priest is coming from out of town for the Liturgy."

"Of course," replied Kalina. "I'll see you tomorrow."

16

CHANTS AND A CHANCE

I wish I had something nicer to wear, thought Kalina to herself as she perused through her wardrobe. She settled on a blouse with a skirt, and she used a scarf as a make-shift headcovering for church. Maura was still showering, but she was adamant that she attend church with Kalina.

"I've heard of Eastern Rite Catholics, but I've never been to one of their masses before," she said to Kalina as they were heading towards the newly built chapel.

"Well it can't be that different from a Catholic mass, right?" Kalina asked.

"You would be surprised," replied Maura. "My mother insists that we go to TLM and not Novus Ordo."

Kalina didn't know what either of those meant, but they had already reached the doors of the chapel. The nave wasn't as ornate as any other Orthodox church she had been to, but there were icons hung on the walls and a makeshift iconostasis for her to venerate. Presumably, they would have to share the space for students of other faiths, but she respected the work Dean Schulz had done in order to build up a proper worship space for her and other students. She prepared herself for the Liturgy by venerating the icon of Christ and signing herself with the cross. Upon bowing down, she made eye-contact with Dr. Toumi, who motioned for her to approach him. He was sitting down on a chair next to the chanter's area, where there was a girl who looked about the same age as herself. Her footsteps clicked on the wooden floor as she approached him.

"Good morning, Kalina. I'd like to introduce you to my daughter, Juliana. She just started school this year."

"Hello, it's nice to meet you," greeted the young, dark-haired girl. "My dad told me that you knew how to chant?"

"Well, I know some of the chants, but I'm not sure whether or not I'll be any good."

"You'll be fine, Kalina," reassured Dr. Toumi. "We just need some people to help with the reading who are familiar with the service. There are more Orthodox students here, who I asked to help. I believe Harris is in your class?"

"He's Orthodox?"

"Yes, he's Lebanese."

Kalina wasn't expecting the blonde-haired, blue-eyed kid named Harris to be from the Levante, but the world was full of surprises. Since they still had about twenty minutes before the service began, Kalina introduced Maura to Juliana and they looked through the hymns together. Although Maura was a talented musician, she had to admit that she couldn't read the Byzantine notation. Although Kalina was in the same position, she was familiar with the sounds of each chant and hymn based on Sunday Liturgy and her own private prayers. Fortunately, Juliana was trained in reading, and Kalina was comfortable enough to follow her lead.

To the average student, the service seemed atypically long while the sermon seemed to be abnormally short. Kalina herself wished she was better at paying attention to the priest's words, but often found her mind wandering. The church was largely empty by the time the Divine Liturgy was finished since many of the students had left after the Eucharist had been delivered, even the ones who partook. Kalina herself didn't normally stay for the end of worship since she would go with other kids to Sunday school after communion. Juliana thanked her before heading over to her dad, who was talking to the priest, leaving her and Maura to talk.

"What did you think of it?" asked Kalina, hoping that her friend received a positive first impression of her faith.

"The choir was really pretty, and I recognized several similar elements such as the Trisagion hymns and the litanies from the Catholic Mass. I also really liked the sermon. I think that the priest was very eloquent."

"Would you come back?"

"I don't know. I should probably keep going to Catholic Mass since that's what my parents are."

"True, I think my parents would say the same about me going to a Latin Mass!"

"Well, if that's it, then I guess we should head out. I'm surprised that a bunch of people left so soon, but they probably got tired - or bored."

The two turned around to exit, and Kalina replied, "I think it's tough for people to wait so long without entertainment or distractions or any sort of noise. Then, it only takes one person to leave before others follow. Have you noticed that Robert Nelson is like that - a natural leader I mean (not lazy), but I think he's genuinely concerned about the well-being of others."

"Yeah," agreed Maura, who pointed to the opposite corner. "He's actually right over there."

"Where?" asked Kalina before looking where Maura had stuck her finger. In the back corner, Robert was talking to Mr. Wells. Suddenly, an idea came to her, and she walked over. "Let's say 'hi.'"

As soon as Kalina and Maura approached, the conversation between the two men died down, and Mr. Wells greeted them.

"Hi, Kalina. You did an excellent job chanting today."

"Oh, thank you, but it was mostly Juliana - Dr. Toumi's daughter. What did you guys think of the service?"

"It wasn't what I expected," replied Robert at first. "It's very different from an Anglican service in a lot of ways - like the singing. I was just talking to Mr. Wells about that actually."

"I thought it lovely," answered Mr. Wells in addition. "The only thing is that I'll have to move from the Old Calendar to the New Calendar if I'm going to continue attending the services here."

Kalina shook her head in surprise. "Are you already Orthodox then or are you a catechumen?"

"I was baptized... several years ago," responded the young teacher. "Didn't you see me taking communion?"

"No," Kalina admitted. "I might have been too focused on the chanting."

"I'd say that's a good thing, Kalina. Well, I should probably be headed home now. I'll see you all later this week."

"Hold on, Mr. Wells!" interjected Kalina, impatient to ask her question.

"Yes?"

Kalina didn't know how to ask her question, so it all came out abruptly.

"Doyouthinkyoucanbemymentor?"

"What?"

"Um... do you think that maybe you could be my mentor?" she repeated more slowly. "You *were* Phillip's, so I figured... since you already have experience with my brother, you could help me with *my* aptitude."

Mr. Wells hesitated before answering. He looked like he wanted to reject her proposition but was trying to find a diplomatic way to say it. Eventually, all he said was "I'll have to talk to Dean Schulz and Dr. Toumi about it." Without saying anything else - not even a good-bye - he turned and brusquely exited the chapel.

"Well that was terse," noted Maura, cutting the silence.

"He was uncomfortable," stated Robert. "I could feel it trickling off of him. I reckon he thinks that your brother's disappearance was his responsibility."

"Of course it wasn't," grunted Kalina.

"And it wasn't yours either," answered Robert, staring intensely at her. "Has anyone told you that yet?"

"I mean... if I hadn't...," began Kalina, but her voice trickled off as she realized the truth of Robert's words. All this time she had been struggling with her role in the fiasco. If she had been more careful or if she had listened to Sister Maryam or if she could just do it all over again. However, she can't, and she felt that it was her responsibility to make everything right.

"He's right, you know," agreed Maura, placing a comforting hand on Kalina's shoulder. It was the last thing she needed. Kalina despised the pitiful look that people gave her.

"Regardless," said Kalina. "We have to find out what happened. If there's anything we can do to find Phillip, we have to do it. Mr. Wells trained Phillip, so he's the one who is most familiar with his aptitude. Maybe he knows something that can be useful to us."

"He's a hard nut to crack, even for me," responded Robert. "And I'm not being arrogant either. Of course, a lot of teachers are able to keep their mental guards up, but I can still feel how fragile some of their walls are."

"Very humble," scoffed Maura. "Besides, I thought that Mr. Wells had a physical aptitude not a psychic one. Doesn't he teach physics?"

"Yeah, but that doesn't mean he's necessarily a physicist. It could just be that that's what he teaches. No one actually knows what his aptitude is."

Maura sighed, "Another mystery, then?"

17

TRADITIONS AND SUPERSTITIONS

Kalina didn't wake up early the following Monday. In fact, she had to be woken up by Maura, who had also slept in by accident. The two were now sprinting across the lawn in order to make it to class on time. Kalina cursed under her breath when they entered the building; the main clock read 8:48, meaning they had already missed all of Homeroom and the first three minutes of Magical Theory and Practice. As they sped down the hall, Maura cupped her hands and let out a hot whisper into it. She placed her hand on the brass buckle of her belt for a few seconds before removing it. The shiny brass caught Kalina's eye, prompting Maura to smugly say, "I *told* you to read the self-care manual they gave us."

Before Kalina could ask for the spell, Maura furtively pushed open the classroom door, and the two shamefully walked in. Miss Haverty, who was handing out their diagnostic quiz from last week, stopped in her tracks to greet them. It was more embarrassing to have her attention on them, but Kalina felt that they deserved it to a degree. This way, the class will forget about them and move on.

"Welcome, ladies. Did you oversleep?" asked Miss Haverty calmly. Maura and Kalina both nodded their heads regretfully. Miss Haverty addressed them before continuing. "Well, sit down and don't let it happen again."

The two roommates gratefully went to their desks to inspect their scores. Kalina, who was somewhat of an overachiever, was dissatisfied with her grade, but the score was what she expected. Her foresight might have helped her in a course like math, but Magical Theory and Practice is specific to her environment. It's no secret that categories, definitions, and vocabulary vary in the magical community across time and space. What might have been correct for Ms. Dalton was not necessarily correct for Miss Havery.

"You guys did very well overall; although, I noticed some inaccuracies in your work. We were worried that Ms. Dalton would have been teaching a lot of prohibited magic, but it seems that she largely played it safe. However, there are some... outdated misunderstandings in your work," explained Miss Haverty in a soft, drawn out tone. Kalina could tell she was exasperated with the work cut out for her this year. "For the most part, you guys did well remembering the high classifications: physical and psychic, Aristotle's elemental classifications... Yes, Alaric?"

"There was one elemental classification that you marked wrong -"

"No, I didn't," she interrupted. "The cryology one, right? Several of you gave wrong answers. Can anyone tell me which classical element type it is?"

Harris raised his hand and answered, "It's a fire type because making something cold requires one to transfer the heat somewhere else. Normally, a cryologist can keep a token to transfer that energy to."

"That is absolutely correct! The manipulation of thermal energy is why cryology is counterintuitively considered pyral. Most of you put water because in medieval times, cryology was considered both cold and wet. However, today there has been a push to use modern science and thermodynamic principles in order to classify magical functions. It's a uniquely Anglo-American phenomenon, but the Virginia Magical Burgess requires that I teach it to you this way. Now, does anyone have any questions on Harris' reasoning?"

Kalina flipped to the question and grimaced. She had written water, and was angry with herself for getting it wrong - even if the answer was correct in another time and country. She wondered if her father had been taught the other way, having been trained in Yugoslavia.

As if reading her mind, Miss Haverty continued, "Many of you wrote water, which makes sense. That's a fairly archaic understanding of this aptitude. Actually a lot of you used outdated terms. I saw a lot of you using '-mancies' and not '-ologies.' A lot of you described geometries as 'sigils' or 'runes,' and those are actually types of geometry or enchantment. Not to mention that 'sigils' are considered to be witchcraft. What's most disappointing is that most of you forgot all seven magical natural wonders of the world, but we'll review that in social studies. Does everyone have their test back? And does anyone have any questions about it? Remember it's not for a grade, just to see what you were taught last year."

One girl in the back raised her hand, but spoke before being given permission.

"Did Ms. Dalton teach us these things because she was a witch?"

Kalina and Maura both shot their heads around; it was Laurelle! They hadn't spoken to her in what seemed like ages, and now she was behaving uncharacteristically: drawing attention to herself by asking a controversial question. The class was in shock, and some even turned their heads to look at Kalina. *They think something happened between me and Dalton*, she thought. *It's alright, Laurelle knows me. She knows that I'm not sensitive about these things. If anything, I'm as interested in how Miss Haverty will answer this question as she is.*

"Everyone knows witches aren't real. That's just a rumor," snapped another student.

Before an argument could arise, Miss Haverty intervened.

"If you all had received a proper education last year, then you would know that Laurelle is right about witches existing. There are two types of witches: those born with magic and those without. That is, there are those born with magic who turn to the prohibited arts: nigromancy, pyromancy, illusion, possession, et cetera. They are as old as humanity itself, appearing in many different cultures. However, in the past couple of centuries the problem has exacerbated and is one of the reasons for AIMM and the growth of magical law enforcement around the world. This took off during the Enlightenment period in Europe, around the sixteenth century when there was a higher interest in the occult and dark arts. Many magi during this period turned dark or were kidnapped by witches, warlocks, and court sorcerers for their magic. Since then, the International Agreement for the Mystery of Magic was signed by many magi representing nations all over the world in order to protect us from people who wish to steal and abuse our natural talents."

Maura raised her hand to ask a question. "What about the Salem witch trials? Were those real witches or not?"

"I actually worked there on an internship for New Amsterdam's Department of Archaeology while I was an undergraduate student in college. It seems that a couple of them might have been, but most of them were probably not, and the genetic testing implied that none of them were magi. Now, if no one else has any questions, we need to transition to mathematics. Does everyone know where they're going?"

The discussion had ended, and Kalina was satisfied to turn to a more stable and reliable subject. However, she was still curious as to why Laurelle was so interested and what Dalton's end goal actually was.

18

BLEACHERS AND BURDENS

The day had turned out to be tiresome given that Kalina had an awkward start to it. She absolutely hated being late, and it threw her off for the rest of the schedule. Despite that, she made an effort to learn about Robert's pastime, sitting on the bleachers after school hoping to learn a thing or two about football. It turned out to be a menial attempt that lasted a mere few minutes.

Kalina had long lost interest in the football team practicing on the field below her. As of now, she was focused on her reading for Magical Theory. She was disappointed in her diagnostic score and felt as though she was behind the rest of the class. To be fair, she had missed forty days of school after being kidnapped. She also had to relearn all the material that Ms. Dalton had led *her* astray on.

"Nice to see you again," greeted the tall, sweaty senior. Robert Nelson was still breathing heavily while climbing the bleachers to the lonely blonde girl with the large textbook on her lap. Below, Kalina could see that the football team had started to disperse. "I'm sorry we didn't have a lot of time to talk yesterday."

"We never did get to talk in depth about the service," commented Kalina.

"It was... interesting. The sermon was very short and the standing was difficult. I had to sit down a few times. Overall, though, I'd say it was a good experience, and I would go back," he replied. Robert himself was a practicing Anglican, but the nuances of religious and theological studies were not matters that deeply interested him. "What are you reading?"

Kalina closed her copy of *Elementary Magical Theory* and presented it to Robert with an exasperated sigh.

"There's so much I need to relearn from last year."

"You don't have to tell me twice. At least you weren't held back an entire year because of a coma."

Kalina winced at Robert, unsure of how to respond. He probably did have it worse than her. Sure, she was kidnapped (and almost killed), but he was knocked into a coma for almost half a year. Who knows what kind of psychological traps and tortures Dalton developed for him while he was unconscious. Then, when he came out of his coma, he found out that his girlfriend started dating someone else and that he had to redo the whole year. *What a mess.* At least now, he was looking a lot more muscular than he was at the end of last year, and Kalina was certain that he'd be quarterback again in no time.

Seeing Kalina's hesitation, Robert sighed and continued, "I'm sorry; I shouldn't have compared myself to you. I know I wasn't in any real imminent danger like you were. It's just that... I don't know how to explain it."

"What's wrong, Robert?" asked Kalina, who perceived that something was troubling him.

He took a seat next to her on the bleachers and said, "I think I'm going to quit football."

Kalina was shocked. Although she didn't really care about the sport, she would never have expected *him* to say anything like that. Robert was more passionate about football than she was about tennis, and she knew how much she relied on the activity to stay sane over the summer.

"What happened?"

"Well, it's not like everything's going back to normal," explained Robert. "Everyone's happy to have me back, but I'm not the quarterback anymore. I'm not even going to be starting at all. Everything's so different now - the plays, the teammates... I didn't think it would change so much. They all made these memories without me; it's like I'm not really part of the team anymore."

Fortunately, Kalina didn't say the first thing that came to mind: *That's why I don't play a team sport.*

"Anyways, sorry to bother you with that," apologized Robert, not that Kalina felt that he had anything to apologize *for*. "How are your classes so far? What elective are you taking?"

"I'm taking choir with Maura. She tested as an acoustician last year."

"Nice, I took art."

"Because of Aisling?" asked Kalina. *Stupid*, she thought to herself. *Why would you bring his ex up?*

"No, we weren't dating yet. I liked to use my telekinesis to make sculptures. How's biology?"

"Hate it."

"That's it?"

"It's boring, and I really dislike -"

"- Mrs. Blackwell," they finished simultaneously.

"She's ancient," said Robert. "She really should retire, but Dean Schulz doesn't want to say anything because she was *his* teacher when he was a student."

Kalina gave a light chuckle before settling down to address more serious matters. She wanted to ask Robert if he had tried making any attempts to find Phillip or Dalton.

"Afraid not," he said. "I think I could find Dalton if I wanted to, but I'm far too nervous about contacting her. As for Phillip, I have tried to search around the intellectual realm, but I haven't had any luck. If you're right that he *has* time-traveled, I'm not even sure how I would be able to reach his conscience. Besides that, I spent the rest of my summer conditioning and practicing for football. The mind and body are intimately connected, you know."

Kalina gulped, "Well, I *had* noticed that you were looking very muscular."

Robert smirked modestly, "Well, thank you."

"I did want to ask you something else, though," continued Kalina. "Last year, I had entered the psychic plane - a sort of hallway, but I haven't been able to access it again. It was very dreamy, and I saw the doors of people who I knew, and I went through some of them. I also think I saw Ms. Dalton, and then guess what? Phillip was there, too, but it was an older version of him, and he saved me. The more I think about it, the more it sounds like a dream. However, I'm certain that I witnessed something genuine."

"Ah, so that was *you*," answered Robert slowly. "I knew I heard someone trying to open my locker! I was afraid it was Dalton coming back for me."

Kalina blinked. "What?"

"Dr. Toumi refers to it as the collective-subconsciousness - not in the Jungian sense, but for me it looks like a series of gym lockers for each person. However, the hallway is the most common manifestation in a person's psyche. The dreamlike state that you mentioned - that's something that you'll overcome the more you practice going in and out of there."

"Okay, I understood the second part... I think."

"Don't worry, you'll learn more about it if you take the psychology classes here. You could also ask Dr. Toumi about it. What's most interesting is considering how it would be possible that Phillip could access it if he's just a teleporter. I thought his type was classified under physical aptitudes. If it's true that he can travel backwards through time -"

"I'm *certain* he has," interrupted Kalina, frustrated at everyone doubting her. "*And* he was a full adult in the... the collective subconscience."

"*Subconsciousness*," corrected Robert. "I'm inclined to agree with you. All I was saying is that if he can travel across time on the physical plane, then maybe one day he'll be able to travel across time on the psychic plane. That would change our whole understanding of cognitive mapping!"

"I think we need to talk to Aisling and Mark," said Kalina abruptly, who didn't think she could handle a psychic nerd-out right that second.

Robert furrowed his eyebrows and nodded his head slowly. There was always something friendly about Robert's composure. Even in the heat of composition, there was always an atmosphere of benevolent sportsmanship. The way his face darkened now reminded her of an eclipsed sun.

"There's something weird between the two of them," he said grimly. "And no, it's not just about their romantic relationship and the fact that she's my ex. I feel like something must have happened between the two of them last year."

"Well, they did enter the Enchanted Forest with Phillip to rescue me."

"And how exactly did they find you?" asked Robert.

Kalina had been so focused on finding Phillip or where Ms. Dalton might be that she didn't consider how it could have been remotely possible for the trio to have found where she was. She took a minute to see if her psychic aptitude could help her connect any dots, but nothing came up immediately - at least nothing positive. Kalina wasn't allowed to see their reports to the police, but she was allowed to see their research report on Enchanted Forest navigation.

"Your right," Kalina finally declared. "Something's not adding up. They said they ran from Dalton, but *she* knew how to navigate the forest. They claimed to have tracked my footprints, but I don't think Dalton would have left any behind. I think they're lying, but I don't know what the truth is."

Robert stared ahead as she spoke, his face as tight as a fisherman's knot. There were no more football players on the field, so for a brief moment, Kalina only heard the rhythmic sounds of crickets. If she could concentrate hard enough, she could see the rhythm of the world, but before she was entranced by it, she forcefully snapped herself back to the worldly plane. She remembered uncontrollably breaking into prophecy last year, and she was too afraid that she would lose herself like that again. Robert didn't seem to notice her inward disposition and continued with his speech.

"Believe me, it's a good thing that you don't have any suspicions of what they were up to; I'd be concerned if you did. I'm fairly certain I know what they used Phillip for, but I want to hear it from their own mouths. We *need* to meet up with them."

19

A COLOR REVELATION

Under a large pine tree adjacent to the stoickee courts, Kalina sat patiently while reading her book. She was used to showing up in a timely manner, which meant that she was also used to waiting for everyone else to show up. Robert was the first, coming from the boys dorm building, while Aisling and Mark came as a couple from the main building. Although she could see them coming in the distance, they were far enough away for her to try the simple incantation from the textbook again.

She pinched her pointer fingers and thumbs together and said, "*Cobalt chroma*" before expanding her fingers into a spadelike arrow. Slowly, the light that traveled between her fingers had turned a deep and vibrant blue. By this time, Robert had finally reached her.

"That's a nice shade of blue. Is that one of Newton's color incantations?" he asked, prompting Kalina to check her book.

"No, it says it's derived from Goethe," she answered. With that, she closed her book and stood up, as Aisling and Mark were just before her.

"Hello, Kalina," greeted Aisling. "Great job on that color spell! I was never good at the ones that required a lot of focus like reds and yellows. You know, the ones with longer frequencies."

"Thank you," replied Kalina, noting Aisling's wild hair, a difference in style compared to Maura's tame locks. It certainly made her pop out on the field when cheerleading. She continued on to greet Mark cordially. "I'm glad you two were both able to come today. We haven't had a chance to catch up yet since school has started. I really wanted to talk to you guys about Phillip and Dalton."

"I'm sorry, Kalina," replied Aisling, with a genuinely apologetic look on her face. "But I think your time-travel hypothesis is the best theory we have so far. Unfortunately, we haven't really had a lot of time over the summer or since school started to explore it any further. In fact, I wouldn't know where to start."

"Maybe you could find Phillip the same way you found Kalina," suggested Robert aggressively, even affecting Kalina for a brief moment. She wondered if he had used his aptitude for emotional impact. It seemed to have worked, as Aisling visibly recoiled and Mark immediately tensed. *What did they do that was so bad that they're behaving this way?* The whites of Aisling's eyes were visible and her hands were trembling whereas Mark stood as still as a statue, looking as though he were holding his breath.

"It's like we told Detective Christie," stated Mark in a voice that so practiced it was almost political. "We had success with navigating the Blue Ridge Enchanted Forest the first time, and we were able to use what we learned to follow Kalina and Dalton, who hadn't left long before we did."

"Don't be terse with me. Your answer was way too quick," pressured Robert.

"And practiced," added Kalina before either Mark *or* Aisling could respond. "You're lying."

"Well, there's no need to thank us," started Mark, turning around on Kalina. "We only put our lives at risk to save you."

"I'm grateful, and I'm certainly not upset. I just want to know what happened - whatever information you're hiding could be related to Phillip's disappearance."

Mark turned towards Robert and asked accusingly, "Have you been looking inside our heads."

"I don't do that," he answered, but his tone seemed to say that he was on the verge of breaking his personal ethical code. "But there's only one way I can think of that could have any chance of reliably getting you to Kalina *through* the Enchanted Forest."

"Why don't you tell us, then," instigated Mark, puffing his chest up. Kalina didn't remember him being so bold, but it seemed to suit him.

"It won't mean anything coming from me," replied Robert. "People would think I planted the idea inside of you."

"Enough of the games," declared Kalina, who was fed up at this point. She reached down within herself to try to find her voice. Doing her best, she commanded, "*Tell the truth.*"

It was nowhere near as powerful as the time the voice came to her when she was escaping Dalton or when she had her aptitude test, but it was affecting Mark and Aisling. Because Mark was resisting so well, she turned her attention to Aisling, who after giving a fight, succumbed to Kalina's stare.

"We used blood magic to find you," she confessed with a wheeze. "We asked Phillip, and he agreed. We were in a time crunch. *We didn't know how long we had!*"

The atmosphere became silent with the sudden release of tension. Mark was torn between staring mournfully at Aisling and glaring at Robert and Kalina. Aisling broke into tears and Mark went to comfort her before Kalina turned to Robert, breaking the silence.

"And the police don't know?" questioned Kalina, whose heart fluttered faster than hummingbird, anxious of the consequences of this major breach in magical law.

"No, and it should stay that way," he answered while Aisling was still sobbing.

"Well, I doubt that. If Robert could see the holes in your story, then a detective definitely could," replied Kalina sternly. She gave Robert a look that said, *I have no idea what to do about this, and I am afraid of my involvement.*

"You had to tell her; Kalina deserved to know," said Robert in a softer voice, even though there was no one close enough to hear them. "Blood magic affects more than one person. It may be the key to understanding why Phillip's anchor didn't work as expected."

"I appreciate the information - and the rescue of course," assured Kalina. "But, I don't think so. If..." She was going to explain that if she could always have seen across both time and space, then it's possible that Phillip's aptitude worked analogously. Although she wasn't sure of the scientific logic behind her statement, she was afraid of revealing too much about her aptitude to Mark and Aisling. It was clear that these two were hiding secrets, and Mark, who she almost considered as a brother, was better at it than Aisling. She could see the ethereal strings connecting them, and then those outside of themselves. Unfortunately, the framework collapsed almost as soon as she started its construction. She simply didn't see enough yet.

"We should go," announced Mark.

He turned around to leave, and Aisling did not hesitate to follow him. The two walked in step like a pair of marching band students towards the main building.

"Well that was odd, but not surprising," said Kalina. Apart from that, she was left speechless.

"You're right, it *was* odd. I would never have commanded Aisling around like that when we were dating."

Kalina shrugged. "What? It's not like that at all. Look at their gait. He's following *her* tempo. Anyways, that's not what I was referring to. There's something else that they're not telling us, but I just don't have enough pieces to the puzzle to figure out the whole picture."

"What do you mean?" asked Robert.

Kalina stared in silence for a while, thinking about how to explain her aptitude to Robert. She had never tried to put her experiences into words before since they were various in degree and type. *I'll start there. It's fortunate that Robert's patient.*

"My aptitude... it manifests itself in different ways. With my little gray cells, I can see things connected together. They tie together like knots on a tapestry or points on a framework. When I have all the pieces, I can see the building or the picture or whatever, but something is missing here."

"Little gray cells... Like Hercule Poirot?"

"You're an Agatha Christie fan, too?"

"Let's not get off on a tangent. If what you're telling me is true, then that means that your aptitude isn't just psychic... you *are* a psychic."

Kalina took a deep breath and sighed. She wished she had longer to keep her secret to herself, but it was only a matter of time before everyone else figured it out. It's not like she could keep her talents to herself despite her efforts. Then, there was that little "noetic" side of her that she wasn't sure to make of. Was it a mistranslation? Or was she naturally predisposed to spiritual matters? As far as she was concerned, she had no saintly enlightened eyes or anything of the sort. She recalled the story of the girl who was able to prophesy by demons in the New Testament and shuddered to consider that she herself might be caught in a similar situation.

"According to Dr. Toumi and Dean Schulz, I'm a 'visionary,' but it's basically the same thing. I'm not really supposed to tell anyone, but you would have found out eventually. You're more educated and powerful than I am."

"Well, if what you're saying is true, then you should take on Dr. Toumi's offer of mentorship. He can really help you learn to harness your aptitude like he did for me."

"No, I don't think so. There's another dimension to my aptitude. Besides, I don't want to talk about Dr. Toumi right now; I have to talk to him every Saturday."

Robert put his hands up in defense. "Well if that's the case, then I should really get going. I have a lot of training and studying to catch up on."

Kalina absently watched him jog off towards the gym before returning to her study on color theory. However, after the recent revelation, she knew she couldn't go back to such a mundane task. *If only there was some way I could practice my aptitude in a more structured manner.*

20

An Eerie Mystery

The clock ticked in the background as four girls studied for their upcoming vocabulary quiz. On the other side of the classroom, Miss Haverty silently sat at her desk, shuffling through papers that needed grading. Kalina was glad that she offered her classroom for her students after school since the library was often crowded and the mess hall was far too loud to do any sort of reading. The only noise was the clock, which Kalina had learned to tune out, and the occasional person coming in and out of the classroom.

"Have you guys worked on the analogies yet?" asked Miss Haverty, who was putting graded sheets of homework into her filing cabinet.

"No," replied Maura. "Last year, we only had to give definitions of the words."

"Our class did the same thing," added Alice, who didn't have Ms. Dalton.

"The vocabulary tests are going to get harder this year. You'll need to know the etymologies, how to use analogies, and you'll also have to use it in a sentence. I know that next year is when you guys will start interpreting incantations," explained Miss Haverty.

"We've got the etymologies and the sentences down," said Kalina. "But we're still working on verbal analogies. I can't wait until we get to ninth grade, when we start *making* our own incantations."

The best convenience about working in Miss Haverty's classroom is that she was always willing to help or answer any question a student might have. She went to the white board and the four girls attentively listened to her as she walked them through various methods of analogy, morphology, and since Maura asked, phonology.

"Well, it's starting to get late. I have to get home, and you guys should get to the mess hall for dinner."

"Hold on," said Olympia, the fourth girl. "Do teachers not live here?"

"No," chuckled Miss Haverty along with the other three girls, who all were walking out of the class. "The dean does, but most of us commute to work. I'm lucky to live in Winterburg since it's relatively close. I'll see you girls next week."

Miss Haverty departed from the path, and the girls had a chance to talk among themselves.

"So, Alice," began Kalina. "What exactly is going on with Laurelle?"

"We've all noticed how she's been acting," prompted Maura. "You told me at hockey practice that you would tell me later. Now's a good time."

Alice's face scrunched up; she was visibly uncomfortable with the topic. She kept her face tense and sullen as she began to explain the situation.

"Well, I'm not really sure where to start. Last year, it felt like the five of us were pretty close, and Laurelle was definitely a part of it. Something must have changed over the summer because Laurelle was never active in our group chat and she never responded to me personally."

"Same for us," interjected Maura, with a light bitterness attached to her voice. Kalina herself was a little hurt that Laurelle never reached out to her, but she hoped that it was because she didn't have access to her phone or a decent signal. "*And* we were her roommates."

Alice glanced at Maura and continued, "I thought that she was just quiet and maybe a little shy or introverted, but she started being kind of short with me at the beginning of the year. Apart from some snide remarks, she's been mostly anti-social in case you haven't noticed. Basically, it's her way or the highway."

"Really? We noticed that she was being socially avoidant, but she never argued with us or anything like that. If anything, she seemed to be somewhat docile," responded Maura. "This year I haven't seen her at all except in class. Kalina thinks that she's jealous."

"*I did not say that!*" snapped Kalina, even though deep down she knew it to be true. Nonetheless, she hated the idea of being an active participant in gossip. "I said that she might have been feeling embarrassed or left out because she didn't get an aptitude whereas everyone else in our friend group did."

Kalina also wanted to add that she understood what it was like to feel cut off from everyone else, to be so ingrained in something that nothing else matters. This is how she treated her friends last year, and she didn't want to reopen old wounds. What she did know was that it took something within herself to be able to mend the relationship: humility.

"It's kind of the same thing," replied Maura, interrupting Kalina's thoughts. "Nobody is hounding her except maybe her parents, but I doubt that. If either one of them cared deeply about whether or not their kids had a powerful level of magic, then each one would have married a full magus - *a powerful one,* too."

It was a harsh saying that caused a couple of the girls to gasp, but Kalina didn't see how she could argue with the logic. Mage-digging wasn't an unknown practice among some families, but it did come with some severe risks. A few people were shallow enough in the magical community to marry into power, and it was a stereotype that only the weakest and most spiteful of them wanted to usurp the strength in order to abuse everyone else. The only problem was that she couldn't picture the Laurelle *she* knew going outside the bounds of law in order to access higher forms of magic. However, there was another side to Laurelle that Kalina had encountered before. Several months ago, she had explored the subconscious activities of various people she knew, and Laurelle's was... *unhinged* to say the least. The school was on fire and she was laughing maniacally. *Did she secretly hate us? If she did*, Kalina countered, *then she did a wonderful job of fooling not only me for a whole year, but everyone else as well.*

"Maybe she's angry at her parents, then," guessed Alice. "Maybe that's why she's interested in wicca."

Every single girl stopped in their tracks at once to look at Alice with ghastly horror splattered across their faces. Maura's face had turned redder than her hair. Olympia's whole body stiffened into a marble pillar. Kalina stared at Alice with eyes opened so wide, she thought for a moment that they were about to fall out.

"You shouldn't spread rumors like that," chastised Olympia in a severe, hushed voice. "Even if she's a nasty, horrible bully, you can't go around accusing people of Artes Prohibitae. My parents are lawyers for MUNA, so I know about this."

"I'm not spreading rumors, and I'm not making any sort of accusations... *Yet*," spat Alice, who seemed as bitter as coffee, and as hot as a fresh cup, too.

At this point, the four girls were huddled in a corner, speaking in whispered tones because they were nervous about eavesdroppers. Even speaking of witchcraft and *Artes Prohibitae* was enough to get them all in serious trouble. In fact, the prohibited arts were the primary reason for the laws on Magical Mystery.

Maura spoke up in a hushed voice, "Olympia's right, Alice. Kalina and I were roommates with Laurelle all year last year, and I can't imagine her getting into any sort of corruptive practices! She's basically a goody-two-shoes."

"I *understand* the gravity of what I said," defended Alice. "The room smells all the time, and she's always drawing these weird symbols from the internet. They're obviously magic, but it's not like the geometric ones we learn about in our art and math classes. They're *different. Arcane.*"

"The room smelling doesn't prove anything," replied Maura. "It could just be that she's trying perfume, or -"

"*No*, it's not that kind of smell. It's a smoky kind of smell... like incense or something herbal, but she casts some sort of incantation so that it doesn't permeate the building or trigger any of the smoke alarms. *I* can still sense it since I live there, and she's getting better at covering it up."

"That still doesn't *prove* anything," asserted Maura. "Tell her, Kalina, Laurelle is quiet and shy; she wouldn't hurt a fly."

At first, Kalina was inclined to agree with Maura and Olympia. Even though they're group wasn't the kind to be exclusionary or mean towards other girls, Kalina was worried that it was happening. However, after Alice's description of Laurelle's covert activities, she couldn't help but be reminded of the techniques that Ms. Dalton employed during their "sessions." The only problem was that Kalina couldn't think of how or when Laurelle would have learned those practices. Ms. Dalton had two thousand years to practice and develop her own esoteric arts, but Laurelle was just twelve. Unless she had access to a practitioner, Laurelle could be putting herself into serious danger by surfing the deep web for unsanctioned spells. Even if she were interested in dark magic, Kalina thought Laurelle to be level-headed enough to approach it 'cautiously.'

"I'm not so sure anymore," Kalina answered finally. "My heart wants to say that you're right, Maura, but what Alice has described has made me suspicious, among other reasons."

"And those reasons would be...?"

"Private," finished Kalina, anxious that she shared too much information already. She didn't want to have to explain that she was poking around in other people's heads. "Come on, we'll arouse suspicion if we stay here all huddled up and secretive for too long."

Without checking to see if the others would follow her, she turned to leave, her mind turning with the possibilities and connecting dots. There were so many times now when she chose to set those theories and conjectures aside. A year ago, she would have been overtaken or overwhelmed by her anxieties and conjectures of the future, but she's stronger now. She can choose to ignore them. Nonetheless, she knew that she would have to eventually contend with this problem facing Laurelle. That much was obvious to her.

21

THE PSYCHIC TRIP

It had been another week at school, and Kalina was starting to become antsy. Not only was her mind circling on the situation with Laurelle, but Mark and Aisling were distant, while Robert was busy with his own schoolwork. *Did no one care about finding Phillip? Did no one care about what happened to Ms. Dalton? There's no way that Mark and Aisling really believe that she's not going to be a problem anymore is there?*

"What's wrong?" asked Maura, interrupting Kalina's racing train of thoughts.

"What do you mean?" replied Kalina.

"You have that look on you. Your eyes become intense and distant, like you're here but not really. I hope you don't distance yourself - I can only deal with one of those at a time. Plus, I can help you know. We are friends after all."

One of the perks of having Maura as a friend was that she was always truthful with you, but never rude. *Tactful*, thought Kalina.

Well, nobody else seems bothered about Phillip or Dalton, so I might as well bring her into the fold.

"Honestly, I'm thinking about my brother and that *hag*. What happened to them? Where are they? And why does it feel like nobody gives a rat's a-"

"Okay, I get it," interrupted Maura. "What can I do to help?"

"What do you mean?" asked Kalina, unsure of whether Maura was talking about helping her emotionally or helping her solve the whole mystery..

"I mean that I'll help you with whatever it is you're going to do. And before you say I can't, I want to remind you that the last time you tried to do things by yourself, you ended up in the clutches of a witch."

"You really mean that? You don't think that I should just leave it to the authorities?"

"Like you said, if no one else seems bothered with it, then nothing will get done. I'm not sure how we're going to figure this out, but I'm sure we can add something to the investigation in a safe way. Besides, why should Aisling get to be the one who has all the crazy adventures?"

They both chuckled, but the uplifting feeling didn't last long. Kalina's body slowly went limp, and she feared that she might be having another seizure. The psychic rush was nowhere near as bad as it was last year, and it didn't last long. Then again, she had been toying with her abilities without supervision and had let her emotions get the better of her. However, the sensation was different - coming from outside herself.. A secondary wave from the intellectual realm had hit her, and she figured out where the origin was.

"Kalina!" shouted Maura, and rushed over her. By the time she reached her roommate, the limpness had left her. "What happened, do I need to call for a medical emergency?"

"No, it wasn't me. It felt like Robert's signature. I think that something's happening to him."

Before Maura could ask any questions, Kalina sprinted out of the room and down the stairs. She could hear Maura tracing her steps and could feel the heightened level of anxiety coming off of her. There was no room in her to take it into consideration, though. Her sole instinctive concern was getting to Robert. She dashed out of the lobby without signing herself out, but Maura quickly did it for them both despite not knowing where they were headed.

As she ran across the field, she could see other students drawn towards the football field in her peripheral vision. *Psychic aptitudes,* recognized Kalina. *They felt it, too.* The ground started to tremble at various intervals, and Kalina saw some other students lose their footing. Despite the risk, she kept moving forward. The tremors exhibited a periodic rhythm whose behavior was predictable.

The second she got to the stadium, the ground had begun to split. Dr. Toumi, Dean Schulz, and a handful of teachers were already there, struggling to contain the students. The mess Kalina encountered brought her to a halt; nothing was where it was supposed to be, giving Kalina the feeling that the whole field was flipped inside out. The grass was uprooted, and the earth cracked. On the sidelines were a group of football players, but it looked like no one was injured.

In the center of the field, lay Robert, shaking. No, he was having a seizure similar to the one she had last year in the library. Only, this one looked even worse, and he was foaming at the mouth like a rabid dog, with his eyes so far back in his head, Kalina couldn't see his pupils at all. Dr. Toumi and Dean Schulz were slowly making their way towards him while other teachers were trying to hold off the amassing crowd.

Suddenly, Kalina was hit with a euphoric wave of psychic energy, and the world melted into the cosmic symphony she had only witnessed a few times before. The past, present, and future melted into one another, and she was pulled by the strings of fate into action. She side-stepped the teachers and maneuvered towards Robert's convulsive body. It didn't take her long to catch up with Dr. Toumi and Mr. Schulz, who were cautiously navigating the psychic and physical entanglements that Robert was creating. It wasn't their fault they couldn't see the pattern, and Kalina doubted that she herself could have been able to just a year ago. The rhythm was complex and jazz-like, seemingly chaotic to the average magus. To Kalina, it was as natural and regular as every breath she took. There was a spiralized path for her to follow, and she moved along it in tempo. Before long, she got to Robert's body, and when she bent down to touch it, the physical world faded away.

This time, she was no longer on the material plane, but inside Robert's consciousness. It looked almost exactly like the Cardinal Key football field. There was a difference, though Kalina couldn't quite put her finger on it. She manifested on the same patch of field, so she wasn't too disoriented. On the other end of the field,

Kalina witnessed a football match, recognizing Robert's jersey as the acting quarterback. *So he still identifies himself that way.* Lest she be trampled, Kalina moved to the sidelines to witness the game, but it didn't merely resemble a competition. She was watching a war. Even though she was familiar with Robert's reputation for passionate plays, what played out before her was aggressive. Both sides were out for blood.

They must be figments of Robert's subconscious, thought Kalina to herself as she watched the two sides line-up for another playoff. *I recognize Jeffreys, and something is familiar about the other team.* Immediately, Kalina put two and two together. The blue and grey jerseys were the same ones as the New England team from last year. In fact, all the players were the same as the ones from that match when Robert was sent to the hospital. Nonetheless, it wasn't a mere memory. That is, it wasn't a replica of the game, but it wasn't spontaneous either. *Like playing Elementafl against a computer*, she reasoned.

Robert still hadn't noticed her, so when the two teams lined up again, she shouted his name. Once, twice, three times. She even tried to summon the voice, but she didn't have the heart for it in this ethereal realm. Still, Robert didn't pay any attention to her. *Who would he pay attention to in a match like this? The coach? The narrator?* Kalina sighed in frustration and cursed to herself. *It wouldn't matter anyways,* she realized. *Neither of them exist here and I don't have the knowledge of how to replicate a different person. Perhaps this is a residual effect of Ms. Dalton's curse - Robert never did go into detail about what he experienced when he was in his coma.*

The game was quickly getting more brutal, but the only person who could get hurt was Robert. *Could he really hurt himself on the psychic plane?* Kalina made another quick examination to see if any of the other players were actually magi fighting Robert. *If I'm right in that they're acting like a computer, then it should be easy to tell who is the human.* Alas, Kalina couldn't see any non-mechanical quirks in the players except for Robert. She turned around slowly in a circle to double-check her surroundings as well to see if anything was off when it hit her. *Nothing is off! It's an idealized version of the stadium.* The sky was fully azure, the field was level and grassy, and the stadium was shiny and polished. In the distance, she could see the gym, which would have locker rooms connected to it.

That's it!

Kalina sprinted towards the gymnasium doors, remembering when Robert told her about how he viewed the collective-subconsciousness. Maybe she could access them from his point of view. If it looked anything like the hallway, she should be able to open a door and let a teacher through - Dr. Toumi. *He knows Robert the best and has a psychic aptitude. He could deal with this by himself or choose to find someone to help him.*

Kalina entered the locker rooms. Fortunately, they didn't smell like the real ones did, but there was another problem she encountered. It wasn't like her hallway, which was infinitely long in only two directions. As she passed the first set of steel gray lockers, she hesitated. It was a maze. A tortuous placement of metal boxes that beckoned her to get lost in.

I'll double check the first set. If he's like me, he'll have the people he's closest to nearest to the entrance. Kalina read the names of his parents, teammates, the coach, Aisling (*still?*), herself... When she saw her own name, she wondered what would happen if she entered. Could she enter her own conscience from here? Where is her conscience right now if not where she is? *Maybe I should accept Dr. Toumi's mentorship. He could probably answer these existential questions.* Finally, she found Dr. Toumi's locker, which was right next to hers and was locked like the others. Kalina took the rotary combination lock in her hand and inspected it.

In her hallway, she could only test the doors to see if they were unlocked. If they happened to be locked, however, she had no hope of getting in. Here, Robert had an advantage, he could theoretically pick the lock or guess the right combination. It was unlikely, though, as Dr. Toumi's lock kept changing symbols. Remembering Robert telling her that he heard someone knocking on his "door," she started pounding on Dr. Toumi's locker, hoping to direct him towards her. Eventually, the lock started spinning by itself, and it dropped to the ground. When the locker opened, Dr. Toumi squeezed through. He was clearly surprised to see her.

"Kalina?" he asked with peaked eyebrows. "How did you find a way in?"

"I don't know. I was just able to do it by instinct. Robert's playing a football game but I can't get his attention."

To anybody else, that would have sounded bizarre. It sounded bizarre to Kalina herself, since she wasn't entirely sure what this all meant. However, Dr. Toumi nodded in understanding and rushed out of the building towards the football field. As he did that, Kalina moved back to her own locker. None of them had designs or patterns like her hallways did, but they seemed to be customized by the lock. *Maybe the secret to entering the doors then is decoding the pattern,* she considered as she inspected her own rotary lock. It was all zeros. She gave it a mere twist and it unlocked automatically. *I suppose I* would *have access to my own consciousness automatically.* The cold, metal door opened and she stepped through, suddenly reentering her physical body.

It took a moment for her senses to adjust as the corporeal world was dimmer in comparison. The skies were gray and the football field was destroyed. *Aren't they supposed to put up wards during practices?* Kalina wondered, looking around. The crowd that had amassed was still there, but Dr. Toumi and Robert were both conscious.

Kalina faced Dean Schulz and asked, "How long was I gone for?"

"Only a few seconds," he replied, stoic as ever. "After you walked up to him, we were easily able to reach him."

Dr. Toumi helped Robert up, and when he saw Kalina, he gave her a puzzled look. He looked tired and his eyes were red. Something about his appearance reminded her of what he looked like at school on his first day back from his coma. Unfortunately he didn't say anything to her, but he and Dr. Toumi walked the other way in order to avoid the students.

"What's going to happen?" asked Kalina.

"We'll get some geologists and surveyors to fix the field. Accidents like this one happen more often than you probably realize. The operation shouldn't take us too much time, but the football team will have to think of something else for practice. The coach will probably have them training weights or doing conditioning."

"I meant about Robert," clarified Kalina.

Dean Schulz sighed, "I can't tell you because it is private. You should go back now; you probably shouldn't have been here in the first place."

After a quick final inspection of the scene, he left Kalina behind to catch up with Dr. Toumi and Robert. In the distance, she could see that Robert's feet were unsteady. There would have been no point in stubbornly following as it would only serve against the benefit of Robert, and she didn't want to cause a raucous.

She didn't want to go through the group of students, either, but decided to do so anyway since she wanted to hear what they were talking about. As she approached however, they started to hush each other, becoming eerily silent. Nevertheless, the lingering sounds of their voices held in the air. She couldn't tell if she was perceiving the past or if Maura was doing it. When she reached her friend, the two headed straight back towards their dorm. Maura was eager to know what happened, and Kalina was happy to share. It was cathartic to have someone to talk to, even if she didn't completely understand the technical workings of psychic magic (although nobody really did).

"So what are you going to do?" questioned Maura. "Are you going to go back?"

"Go back?"

"To the collective-subconsciousness."

"It could be dangerous," replied Kalina, thinking of Dalton's presence. She left out some parts of her first journey, namely when she had invaded Maura's privacy. "But you're right I should learn. Dalton was there. Phillip was there. Robert knows how to use it. He might be willing to teach me. Him or Dr. Toumi perhaps."

Kalina stopped immediately in front of the girls' dormitory, causing Maura to come to a halt as well. Despite early autumn's light breeze and cloudy skies, Kalina felt a light sweat on her forehead.

"What's wrong?" asked Maura.

"I'm too worked up after all that to go back to studying. I need some food to recover and I need to work this out," asserted Kalina, who felt her stomach start to rumble. She must have used up a lot of magic while at the football field and was glad to have eaten a large lunch.

"You get like this often," commented Maura.

"What do you mean 'like this?'" asked Kalina, who was amused. "Do you mean hungry?"

"Well," began Maura, as they headed towards the mess hall. "I mean that you get stubbornly interested in something and can't let it go. At first, it kind of reminded me of my sister, but she's more fleeting about it. If I had to make a comparison to the four elements, I would say she's aerial in her approach. To her, it's almost like a sport, not to belittle her works."

"And for me?" asked Kalina, who was now intrigued with Maura's perceptive analogy.

"You, well you get dead serious about it. It's almost sullen and stubborn. It's like once the fire starts burning you can't put it out until you've made the issue come to light."

"Are you implying that my aptitude is pyral in nature?"

"That kind of analysis is above my paygrade. Maybe I'm just being silly," she answered, and the two walked through the doors of the mess hall.

22

A SUBTLE BUBBLE

DOODOODOO DooDooDoo doodoodoo

Kalina breathed a sigh of relief and walked over to her phone to turn off the alarm and log in her practice hours. *I should call or text my mom*, she thought. *It might make her happy to know that I'm keeping up with my tennis practice this year. Two miles of running plus thirty minutes of wall practice.*

Kalina packed up her tennis equipment and left the court. She had been worried when Dr. Toumi canceled her session this Saturday. Of course, she had complained about the unnecessary appointment beforehand, but now she was concerned with Robert's well-being. However, the other problem she faced was that she didn't know where he was at all. She tried the nursing office, looked all over school, and even went to the football practice on Monday. Moreover, he wasn't responding to any of her texts. *He's either avoiding me or just hasn't been able to reach back out to me yet.* She grimaced when she made that thought, unsure of which of the two she'd rather believe. *I'll just have to try the collective-subconsciousness again*, she thought to herself.

"Why the long face?" asked Maura, who had also just finished practice and caught up with Kalina.

"I'm just concerned about Robert. That's all."

"I'm sure he's fine," comforted Maura. "He was conscious when they left the football field, *and* he was walking."

"You're right. He's probably just been busy. I hope he didn't get in trouble for the damage he caused. How was field hockey?"

"Alice spoke to us again about Laurelle."

Kalina didn't like where this was going. Maura no longer had the edge against Alice in her voice. Instead, she intoned with deep consideration, as though the weight of her following words would be too much for either of them to carry.

"Well, don't leave me in suspense," pushed Kalina, who had a feeling she already knew what her friend was about to tell her.

Maura took a deep sigh, and Kalina had to give her a few seconds in order to gather her thoughts.

"Honestly, it's better if we talk to each other in the privacy of our dorm. One of the older girls told me something about a sound muffler that I want to try. She's not an acoustician; she's a phonologist."

"What's the difference?" asked Kalina.

"Weren't you paying attention at all in choir? Acousticians deal with sounds, vibrations, et cetera. Phonologists deal specifically with sounds of speech. They're like the physical form of scribes - or linguists. My mom's actually a phonologist."

"It's crazy how genetic aptitudes are," commented Kalina, wondering specifically how her clairvoyance, Phillip's teleportation, her mother's physics, and her father's mathematics were all related.

They soon approached the large brick building and signed each other in. Maura let Kalina take the first shower since Kalina didn't like to waste time or water. Meanwhile, she could start researching the sound muffler. When Kalina finished, Maura handed her the project to read about while she took her time.

Fascinating, thought Kalina as she scrolled through the pdf. The recipe Maura had pulled up was meant for a sound-proof dome - not the wall that Kalina imagined. It started with a process of dehumidification. The spell then called for one person to constantly hum a soft tune in order to make a layer of air that would absorb the sounds not of that pitch. This person would be the center of the dome and could control how large the sphere would be. *That's going to be a problem. Maura's the better singer, and she's the one who needs to tell me the information.* The next layer would be a thin sheet of extremely cold air, which Kalina doubted Maura could do. The third and final layer would serve to transmute the energy of any remaining sound into an even layer of kinetic energy. Finally, Maura exited the shower, and a wave of steam left their bathroom. The fact that Maura tended to use up all the hot water was another reason that they agreed on Kalina going first.

"You might want to close the door," said Kalina. "Apparently, we have to dehumidify the room."

Maura obeyed and asked, "What else did you learn?"

"That this spell is going to be impossible for us to do. The second step calls for a hummer to set the absorption of the first layer."

Maura bent down and read the recipe.

"Pff, that's easy. We'll just play a cello drone from YouTube. Also, that layer isn't meant to absorb the sound. It's meant to transmute it into the same pitch. That way the kinetic energy that's released in the third layer is even. I wonder what it feels like."

"I imagine it would be a soft breeze."

Maura nodded in agreement, and the two girls moved to set up their dome. It didn't take too long. The dehumidification process took the most amount of time since they had to look up how to do it. By the end, they had filled up Maura's entire water bottle with air. Neither of the girls liked the feeling of the dry atmosphere since they were both used to the swampy climate of the Chesapeake area.

The two girls worked their way inwards starting with the third layer. They had to work silently, since whenever they spoke, it would disturb the room's atmosphere. The polar layer was then set up with some difficulty. The incantation advised not to voice the spell, but since neither of the girls were thermologists, they had found it almost too strenuous to manage. Kalina felt that she was better than Maura at the nonverbal incantation, but Maura was more powerful when she spoke. Finally, Maura easily set up the pitch-dome and played around with it before their conversation began. In total, it took about eighteen minutes.

"Well, that was fun," said Maura. "But now we have business to talk about."

"Is Laurelle in so much trouble that we had to set all this up."

"Yes," replied Maura gravely, but Kalina had a feeling that she just wanted to try an acoustic related spell. "Alice claimed more adamantly that Laurelle is involved with normie magic."

"You mean wiccan magic?"

"Don't get all politically correct on me," sighed Maura, exasperated. "Say what you want about Alice, but she's not a liar. She told me and *only* me that she had gone through Laurelle's stuff -"

"That's awful!" hissed Kalina, angry about the invasion of privacy. She was about to continue before realizing the hypocrisy of her statement. The secret of invading her friends' psychic spaces was eating at her own conscience.

"*Shhhh!*" scolded Maura. "This dome muffles sound. It's not completely soundproof, and you don't want to destabilize it. As I was saying, Alice claims that she found a grimoire, with occult rituals and everything."

"So what? You can get one of those at any bookstore. You can't walk through Hornes & Goebel without being bombarded by all that nonsense."

"Not this book. Alice described it as being old with ancient diagrams and spells. She couldn't read it, though, because it was all in Latin. Not only that, but there was some sort of necklace which she claimed was a talisman and a bundle of incense."

"Frankincense? Because my parents sometimes use frankincense for prayers," stated Kalina.

"Yeah, I'm Catholic, so I get what you're thinking, but that's not the situation. I know that you're trying to defend her to the best of your ability, but it's worse than we think," replied Maura. "Alice described it as a bundle with one side charred off."

"You don't think she was using pyromancy to light it, do you?"

"I don't know. Probably not. Hopefully not," answered Maura. "But you have to admit that it's not a good look. Laurelle has clearly been caught up with someone who likely groomed her into these practices. There's no way that she could be able to access all of this by herself. Besides, if she hadn't had help, she probably would have gotten hurt by now."

The two girls sat in silence for a few seconds considering the weight of Maura's words and what that would mean for the two of them. Kalina was trying to piece everything together, including her vision of Laurelle's hysteria at the start of summer break. *Could that have anything to do with this?* Kalina considered sharing the circumstance with Maura, but that would raise the question of whether Kalina had invaded Maura's privacy as well. Kalina didn't want to lie to her best friend, but she didn't want to divulge any information either, especially about her aptitude. At this point, it was an open secret she was a psychic, but not everybody knew what she could do.

"Well that's all I have... Unless you have anything you want to share," prompted Maura.

"No, but I'm wondering who could have gotten to her and how," said Kalina, shaking her head. Of course, there was the instance when she walked in on Laurelle in that infernal scene before the summer, but that whole store was a can of worms that she wasn't prepared to open. It couldn't have been Dalton, who had been sent on the run. It might have been that Laurelle had reached out to somebody, a consideration that pained Kalina to think about since it meant that Laurelle would have to be an active party in her pursuits. "Let's take the dome down and get something to eat before the mess hall closes."

The girls merely had to poke and prod at the dome for it to collapse, and before they headed out they rubbed their hands and faces in lotion. The girls sullenly walked the path, the navy skies matching their temperament. The grass was still green and the trees had only barely started to turn color, but one could tell that autumn would descend upon them at any moment. That's how it worked in the Virginias. One minute it would feel like summer, and then the next, you would be hit with the chilly breeze of fall.

The mess hall had its standard variety of food today: meats, salads, sides. They only baked fresh desserts on the weekends, but soft-serve was available everyday at dinner. (Except for last year, when someone tried to cast a spell on the machine in order to get ice-cream for breakfast. It ended up being broken for a couple of months afterwards.) There was always an abundance of food to eat for students who burned calories practicing magic, and an assortment of carbohydrates was never amiss.

"So what are you going to do about Robert?" asked Maura, as she cut up her grilled chicken into bite-sized pieces.

Kalina gulped down her baked potato before responding. "Why do I have so many problems? Laurelle, Robert, Phillip, my family..."

Maura's face twisted in an almost judgmental way. "You're not the only one with problems, Kalina. We're all concerned about Laurelle, Robert, and Phillip plus our own personal matters."

Kalina raised her eyebrows at the last part of Maura's claim. *I've never heard her imply or talk about herself having problems. She's always tried her best to put on a positive persona.*

"Oh, I'm sorry," said Kalina with the softest and most apologetic voice possible. "What's been bothering you?"

"Nothing specifically," said Maura, clearly trying to shrug off whatever triggered her. *She doesn't know that I saw her family*, thought Kalina, who was beginning to think that what she witnessed wasn't an anomaly. "It's only that you sometimes act like you're the center of attention. That you're the only one involved with anything or has any sort of issues that need to be solved. You've got some sort of a mixture between main-character syndrome and a messiah complex."

Hurtful, but somewhat true. Even if she slightly exaggerated my worldview, I can't deny that I do end up making myself the center of attention. I don't think I mean to do it, though. Kalina thought about defending herself, but Maura *did* have a point. She would have to be humbler about her actions in the future. Besides, there was no point in starting an argument over her heated statements when Kalina could clearly see something was eating at her heart.

"I'm sorry," started Kalina, trying her best to be empathetic. "I don't want to keep everybody on the outside like I did last year. Also, if you have anything that you want to address, you can tell me. I know what it's like to keep my issues to myself."

That might work, Kalina praised herself. *I apologized and prompted her to talk about whatever her family is going through in one sentence.*

However, Maura just shrugged, "No, no. *I'm* sorry. I think I'm just frustrated and stressed between classes and Laurelle and Robert and everything. I didn't mean to take it out on you."

Kalina looked around the mess hall to see if she recognized anyone. Although disappointed that Maura wouldn't open up, she was pleased that they smoothed everything over. Confrontation doesn't necessarily have to be aggressive, and it is usually the best solution to any existing problem. In the corner of her eye, Kalina caught a poof of red locks accompanied by a young man capped with sandy hair. The two had exited the mess hall hand-in-hand.

"I think I just saw your sister leave with Mark," said Kalina.

"Good riddance," spat Maura, surprising Kalina. "I can't stand the two of them right now. They're grossly inseparable. I ask Aisling if she wants to have lunch. '*Sure can Mark come along?*' I ask her if she wants to meet up. '*Yeah, Mark and I are close by.*' It's insufferable."

Maura had been stabbing her food with her fork, and she finished by placing all the stacked food in her mouth. It was almost too much for her to fit in there, and Kalina thought she looked like a chipmunk as she struggled to chew it all.

"How do your parents feel about their relationship?" asked Kalina, and patiently waited for her friend to swallow before she could answer.

"I already told you. They're fine with it. We're not ultra-conservative - we're allowed to date. It's not like Aisling's going to get an arranged marriage."

"Oh, I just meant that you guys are Catholics, but Mark isn't."

Maura squinched her face up. Kalina knew then that she had hit some sort of nerve.

"*Are you asking that because my dad was in the IRA? Aisling needs to keep her mouth shut,*" hissed Maura.

"The tax thing?" asked Kalina, confused as to what sort of trigger caused Maura to become so irate. Since her dad was a mathematician, he used to work on individual retirement accounts. It was tiresome work for him, but never stressful. As soon as Kalina had asked for clarification, Maura's face softened.

"Oh, no, not that," she quickly stated, trying to distance the conversation from her momentary outburst. "Never mind. It's true that both my parents attend church regularly, but they're not extremely zealous about it. However, I do think that they hope Mark would convert if the two ever get married."

Kalina nodded in understanding. She was sure that her parents would feel the same way if she were ever to get married. She snickered at the thought.

"What's that for?" asked Maura in response.

"I was just thinking about how my parents would react if I marry. It's just so far in the future that it seems silly to think about."

"You mean you've never thought about what you would want for your wedding day?" asked Maura.

Kalina pondered for a moment before responding. "I guess I'll have it at church with friends and family. Beyond that, I haven't really considered it any further."

Maura just shrugged. "I have, but maybe I'm the weird one then."

The two finished up their plates and fed them to the clean up system before heading back to their dorm. By now, it was much darker, and the crickets were singing louder.

"You know," Maura began. "I was thinking about Robert and how you two might be able to communicate. You said you were using binaural beats at one point, right?"

"I've been warned against them, but I think I'm experienced enough now to start using them responsibly. A specific frequency can allow me to access the right state," considered Kalina, who was now tempted to go back into her old habits. *In any case, I would have Maura watching over me,* she justified to herself.

"Well, that's just it. I was wondering if we could play around with the frequencies to see if they could lead you to different places or experiences. It could help you find Phillip and Ms. Dalton also."

"That's a brilliant idea," exclaimed Kalina, who was all in. "As an acoustician you could control the sound, but I guess you'd have to do it from the strict standpoint of musical theory."

Kalina frowned at the thought of having to calculate all sorts of wave functions and researching various chords and scales. She kicked a rock into the grass out of frustration

"You say that as though it's a limiting factor," continued Maura, who was more excited about the chance to put her aptitude and her interests into use. "But it expands the opportunities we have rather than just winging it. I could get out my textbook tonight and we can practice harmonizing."

Kalina, glad that someone was optimistic about what she thought to be the boring part, opened the door to the girls' dorm building for Maura and smirked.

"Is this one of your ploys to get me to practice for choir?" she teased.

"No, I'm serious. Although, I suppose that would be an added benefit. Believe me, you don't have the worst voice in our choir."

"Thanks?" responded Kalina to the backhanded compliment.

The two girls excitedly signed their names in and greeted Mrs. Donna before rushing up the stairwell to their dorm and opening up their books. This would be the second time this evening practicing magic, but their dinner was plenty enough to fuel their experiment. As they walked down the corridor, Kalina imagined that she sensed a faint aroma of smoke. Before they entered their room, they greeted Stephanie, who herself was likely to be headed to the mess hall.

"What kind of trouble are you two up to?" she asked with narrow eyes. "I hope it's nothing too serious; there are weird rumors spreading about your class. And some of you are acting... suspicious."

Kalina and Maura looked at each other. Stephanie was normally nice - cool, even. Then again, she rarely had to exercise her authority on the girls. Last year must have changed things, and for the first time, Kalina considered what consequences her actions may have had on Stephanie.

"Nothing," answered Maura a little too nonchalantly. "We're just getting back to our studying and... yeah."

Stephanie squinted her eyes at them.

"Hmm... alright then," she added. "One more thing, casting a sound-proof dome is only going to get more people to pay attention to you. It's not as subtle as you think it is."

"We were practicing for choir class and didn't want to disturb the floor," responded Maura without missing a beat.

"Okay," said Stephanie in a tone that made it clear that she didn't believe their excuse.

Their peer mentor turned away and headed down the stairwell, and Kalina felt a memory trickle through her mind - a younger version of Stephanie inside a similar dome with a group of girls. While Maura's heart raced and her breath labored, Kalina chortled.

"What's so funny?" asked Maura as she opened their door. "We could have gotten in trouble. And what about those rumors? Do you think she's talking about Laurelle?"

"I'm laughing because she's obviously done it, too - that's how she knows. We aren't the first ones to try it, and we're probably not going to be the last."

Maura broke into a humorous smile, bearing her ivory teeth once Kalina placed the dots for her. The two then set up a plan for which tones at which frequencies they were going to attune to. Maura wasn't as skilled at the trigonometry required, but Kalina had mathematics in her blood and effortlessly calculated the wave properties. Although the frequencies were most important, they had to figure out the proper amplitude and timbre. She climbed into her pristine bunk, and closed her eyes, trusting Maura to guide her meditation.

23

CRACKS IN THE CONSCIENCE

Kalina awoke in the school library. It wasn't fuzzy like a dream, nor was it the actual library. Just like Robert's football field, this was an idealized version of the Cardinal Key book collection; the clarity was an improvement since her summertime reverie, and she wondered if Maura's humming made a difference in the experience. Her first instinct was to exit the room and find Robert's personal library, but she hesitated for a moment. Instead, she decided to give the books and tomes a closer look to see if she could read any of them. In the past, the dreamlike realm had been too faded and foggy for Kalina to bother paying attention to the minutiae, but her visit to Robert's psyche gave her an idea. Like the locks in Robert's subconsciousness, some of the titles had mysterious shapes and letters on them. There was one that had fluid, melting Arabic script engraved over its cover, and Kalina wondered if it was related to Dr. Toumi. Most of them, however, were written using the Latin alphabet, though most weren't in English.

No, realized Kalina after a double-take. Several of the letter combinations were too odd for it to be a foreign language (except for the consonant heavy Polish). *It* is *English (probably), but it's written in some sort of cipher.* If Kalina's dad were here, he would be instantly able to name the ciphers used for each of the books, which opened up easily unlike the lockers. *If this library is anything like Robert's locker room, then the people I'm closest to will be closest to the entrance - no, the desk. That's where I manifested this time and last time,* she remembered.

She turned towards the front desk, where a school librarian would normally be seated and was amazed to see a stack of books already there. Kalina smirked in delight. *This is almost too easy*, she thought to herself, looking at each of the covers. Even though she couldn't necessarily read the titles, the cover pages featured similar designs to the doorways she encountered. The one on top had an advanced design of a series of concentric rings layering over each other. Unlike the plaque, it was colored with reds, violets, and blues in an abstract manner. The title read *Ymgdm Pazahmz*. Kalina grinned wider; it was a twelfth rotation shift for *Maura Donovan*.

Quickly, she looked around for a pen and paper and began writing down the shift. She then opened the first page of the book and applied her key to the text. After she had decrypted the first few words, the rest were automatically transmuted into plaintext. However, Maura wasn't who Kalina was looking for - plus she didn't want to further trespass on her privacy. Right now, she needed to figure out what was going on with Robert.

Looking through the stack of books, she found another cover that was familiar to her. She wouldn't have recognized Robert's book if it weren't for the nordic inspired interlace border. The middle depicted a medieval knight on horseback with his sword raised to the air. It was gorgeous, but the real kicker was the title. It shifted between squiggles and letters and other glyphs that she had never seen before. Not knowing where to start, Kalina opened the book to see if she could get any more hints, but every time she flipped a page, it changed. When she went back to the first page, it also changed.

"Are you reading anything interesting?" asked a voice, causing Kalina to jump in fear.

The last time she had been here, Dalton had found her and tried to attack her. This time, however, it was only Robert.

"How did you get in here?" questioned Kalina. "You told me once that you couldn't get in my mind. Have I gotten weaker?"

"No, you've gotten stronger, but so have I. That doesn't really have anything to do with it, though. You let me in."

"What do you mean?" asked Kalina. "You let yourself in! And what do you mean by 'getting stronger.' What happened at the football field? Where are you? What are you doing?"

"Geez, I should have expected this. I'll answer one question at a time," he said. He then shook his head and sighed. "I sometimes forget how inexperienced you are despite your level of magic. For your first question, this is very important to understanding psychological magic. *A door allows for two-way entries.* When you open up a path to enter someone's mind, you have to be careful because you may have also opened up access to your mind from *their* end - even if it was unintentional."

Kalina nodded in understanding, remembering when she had allowed Dr. Toumi to enter Robert's mind by pounding on his locker.

"Okay, two questions, then," began Kalina. "First of all, are these books conceptually doors, then? If so, what happened to the real doors?"

"Good question, and I actually had to walk through my door to get into the library."

He then hesitated a long time before continuing. Kalina didn't want to interrupt him because she knew that he was searching for the right words to answer her question.

"It's so hard to really describe the mechanics of psychology because it *isn't* a mechanical or technical science like physics or chemistry. It's fluid and perceived a little differently by everybody. My best guess is that your books act as... keys? Maybe they're also a sort of map? I think that the reason I was able to find my way towards this library was because you were reading my book over here, and I was drawn to it. I'm not sure I have an exact equivalent on my end."

Kalina looked at the other books that she laid out over the wooden desk. Now that Robert was here, she saw them with more clarity - with another perspective and wondered if Robert picked the locks the same way she could decrypt the books.

"I was also listening for you. I figured you would try to reach out to me. You were right, by the way. That's why they took me back to Saint Luke's."

Kalina was barely following what Robert was saying. *No wonder there's so much dispute on nature and laws regarding psychic magic,* she reflected in frustration.

"You're going to need to be more specific, Robert," she demanded.

"Well, remember when you told me that a part of me was missing? You were right. I had some sort of wall - a psychic barrier to keep my aptitude in check. I was never aware of it, and I don't think Dalton knew what it was because she must have taken it down."

"Why would she do that?"

"She probably thought it was a defensive barrier. In fact, she probably saved me from herself by doing that. Without a heightened level of power, I might not have been able to hold her off. I may have even succumbed to her attack permanently," he said regretfully and with the same gratitude for life that seeps into men who have had near death experiences.

He looked downwards, pensive. Kalina knew that feeling, being on the edge of the afterlife. If things hadn't gone right this way or another, neither she nor he would have been here in the present. However, it *did* work out for the best, and Kalina could only hope and trust that God meant to have it that way.

"Who would do that to you?" asked Kalina, upset at the thought of anyone trying to put a magical muzzle on her. "Who would inhibit your power like that? That's like cutting out a singer's tongue or breaking a painter's fingers."

Robert sighed, "My parents did, and I don't blame them for it. To be honest, I was upset at first, but I realized why they did it and

I believe that they truly had the best intentions. When I was a child, my aptitude was out of control... it *controlled* me. I would suffer headaches and epileptic seizures. All that pent up magic inside me had to be let out somehow, and the aftermath was always explosive. I think... I think I hurt someone once, but that memory hasn't returned to me yet, and my parents keep denying that anything like that happened."

Of course Kalina understood the feeling of being swayed by the whims of her own aptitude, but she had always fought to maintain control. Even when it was at the brink of taking over, she always found a way to master it in the end. It made for an awkward relationship between her and her aptitude.

"I don't want the same thing to happen to you," said Robert. "I know how you keep your abilities hidden, but I can tell that you have an intense power. Perhaps even beyond mine. You really should consider getting a mentor, especially if you want to find your brother or protect yourself from Dalton. I'll be back at school by the beginning of next week, but I'll have to catch up on everything I've missed."

"And the football team?" questioned Kalina. "What about that? Are you going to get in trouble?"

"No, I spoke to coach and Dean Schulz. No one blames me for what happened. If anything, Dr. Toumi - Dr. Toumi's wife I mean - felt guilty that she wasn't able to catch the anomaly in my psychological space. That being said, I did resign from the football team. Coach wanted me to stay, but I can tell that the team has outgrown me..."

He said it stoically, but Kalina was sure that it hurt him terribly to say that and to have to believe it. Robert had put his heart and soul into football, but now he had felt that it was for nothing. Kalina, though introverted, never had that problem *specifically*. Apart from glimpses of foresight, her aptitude allowed to see how the world fit together. Even when she was in her anti-social phase, she knew her place. Robert, however, had tried to jump back in the river only to find it flowing in a different direction.

"I see," began Kalina, unsure of how to respond to that. "You could always try a solo sport like me. I play tennis."

Robert smiled at Kalina's attempt to lift his spirits.

"I might take you up on that offer," he said. "I have to go now, though. It's probably time for dinner."

He turned to leave, but Kalina stopped him.

"Hold on! I want to try something."

Kalina grabbed Robert's open tome from the desk and with as much force as possible, snapped it shut. Immediately, the whole vision dissipated and she was brought back to her earthly dormitory. Maura had still been singing the two tones, but stopped when she saw Kalina sit up.

"Well that was short," she noted. "Were you unable to... pass over? What's the right term?"

"Entering the psychic plane... maybe..." answered Kalina. "And no, I was gone for a while there. How long has it been?"

"Only five minutes. I was worried that you wouldn't be able to make it each time I had to catch my breath."

"That's incredible!" exclaimed Kalina. "In the past, my visions took too long for such a short amount of information, but I can economize my time now."

"That... makes sense," claimed Maura, uncertainty reverberating through her teeth. "What happened and what do we do next?"

Kalina explained the sojourn, including the part where she had found Maura's book. There was no way Kalina could get her help without telling her the whole truth - or most of it at least. Since Maura would have found out anyway, Kalina figured it would be best to be transparent from the start. Still, she didn't confess her very first invasion of Maura's mind, where she thought she witnessed -

No, Kalina interrupted herself internally. *Maura and Aisling are so nice and extroverted. There's no way their home life could be that rough.*

Pushing those thoughts to the side, along with the itch of soothsaying, Kalina and Maura worked together with a framework of a plan to find Phillip and Dalton. Of course, they would need to talk to Robert - ask him questions, and also find a way to talk to Aisling and Mark.

"Are you okay Kalina?" asked Maura. "You're scratching yourself pretty roughly."

"I'm fine," shrugged Kalina, who looked down to notice that Maura was right. She had been itching her arms and legs, turning them dry and red. "I guess, I'm just a little itchy."

Kalina tried to control her impulse, but she couldn't help it. She collapsed to the ground and had a seizure while Maura called for a medical emergency.

24

SECRETS AND REGRETS

The vision was short and flashy this time, as if her magic were charging Kalina for using so much of it in such a short period. Despite the brief succession of images, she had lost all consciousness, leaving her to wake up in the nurse's office hours later. Quickly, Kalina tried to remember everything that she saw before she forgot them all.

Phillip - he was walking into the school library then vanished.

The other library - the one she had been tossed into when she had disappeared for over a month.

Mr. Wells - emerging from... the ground?

Maybe that last one was just a dream, thought Kalina, though she couldn't help but wonder if it was related to why he was asked to train Phillip. *No one knows what his aptitude is. It has to be something related to traveling somehow. But then why didn't Dean Schulz have Mr. Rumsey tutor Phillip? He's supposed to be the navigation and cartography expert.*

"Oh, you're awake," noted the nurse, interrupting Kalina's train of thought. "I'll go get Dr. Toumi, I'm not as good with mental maladies."

"Um, okay," replied Kalina, embarrassed that she had never learned the nurse's name. She had only spoken to Dr. Toumi, given the nature of her aptitude (and the fact that she didn't often get sick or injured).

It didn't take long for the nurse to emerge from Dr. Toumi's office with the man himself. He was clearly stressed about her condition, and Kalina knew that she was going to hear a lecture one way or another.

"My parents?" Kalina asked, already knowing that they had been informed.

"Yes, don't worry. I've already spoken to them, and they're already on their way. You were out all night."

"I know. I can read it on your face," remarked Kalina, trying to be lighthearted. Dr. Toumi, however, maintained a serious demeanor. It was bad enough that Robert had a seizure not too long ago, but a second student under his watch was now facing similar symptoms.

"This is no small matter, Kalina. We can't have you passing out at school. Last year, I thought you just fainted due to the stress of your environment. Maura told us what you two were up to, and it is my belief that you need professional training to deal with your aptitude. Instead of our typical Saturday session this morning, we're going to have a meeting. You, me, and your parents."

Naturally, Kalina's parents arrived as early as they could, but she was still far too tired to have a deep conversation with them. After talking briefly to their daughter and Dr. Toumi, Catherine and Ivan decided to find a motel to stay the night in Winterburg. They would come back later, when Kalina had gotten enough rest, to sit down in Dr. Toumi's office in order to have a discussion about Kalina's welfare and aptitude. As Kalina laid in bed, she struggled to flesh out her prior visions, but her head remained stubbornly empty. Most people would have been jealous of the peaceful clarity, but it only made Kalina frustrated that she couldn't conjure up any sort of contemplations ex nihilo. She figured that she had used up all her mental capacity during her psychic escapade. Eventually, she fell asleep in the nurse's hall while counting to a thousand.

***

The sun was at its apex by the time Kalina was awake again, and her first instinct was that she would be late for class again. Even on the weekends, she set an alarm for herself as she never liked sleeping in. Remembering her surroundings and the date, she calmly crawled out of bed and headed to Dr. Toumi's personal office. There, she found her parents already present and talking to Dr. Toumi, but they fell silent when Kalina walked in. Clearly, their trip to Winterburg was a success, and they were likely to stay for church tomorrow morning.

"You're awake!" exclaimed Dr. Toumi. "Have a seat, we were just talking about a diagnosis and steps to take in order to prevent another seizure."

"Good morning," greeted her mother (somewhat ironically), standing up to give her a hug. Likewise, her father stood up to embrace her. Kalina noticed that the two looked more invigorated since the last time she saw them, which surprised her. All these weeks, she was worried that they would become more and more despondent, yet here they stood, with more color in their cheeks and straighter statures.

"Well," began Dr. Toumi. "I was speaking to my wife about this, since she's a doctor, and we believe that these seizures may be a result of Kalina's aptitude."

"Oh," replied Catherine Todorova. "Last year, we thought that it was due to the stress of a new environment."

"Last year, we didn't know about her aptitude," answered Dr. Toumi.

"And we still don't know what it is," added Ivan Todorova with a raised eyebrow.

All three of them looked directly at Kalina, who could only bring herself to shrug.

"You didn't tell your parents Kalina?" asked Dr. Toumi. "Why not?"

"I just wanted to keep it private, I guess," said Kalina. "Besides, given the circumstances, it didn't feel as important."

"Do you mind if I tell you parents, Kalina?" asked Dr. Toumi.

Kalina sighed, "No, I can tell them myself... I'm a 'visionary' - basically, I have precognitive abilities."

Both her parents started nodding their heads, as if it all made sense.

"Well, actually that doesn't surprise me," stated Catherine Todorova. "She always seemed to be prepared for any circumstance and is very hard to surprise. It also makes sense from a genetic standpoint - Ivan's a mathematician, my brother is a statistician - they're often working with regression, derivatives, and other predictive methods. If Phillip can move across space, then it's also fitting that Kalina can see across time."

"I can see across space, too," added Kalina, implying that Phillip could likewise travel across time.

Her father, however, had a different perspective. "Is foresight not witchcraft?" he asked skeptically.

"In this case, not technically," replied Dr. Toumi. "It's certainly a tricky question, and like I always say, psychic aptitudes, or rather aptitudes of the intellect as they are more recently being called, are much trickier to define. Research on them is still very slow since it's difficult to measure them empirically. The kind of magic you're thinking about involves superstitions like horoscopes, astrology, and the I, Ching - or worse, connection to spirits in the form of possession."

"Hmm..." considered Kalina's father. "I'm not sure how I feel about this yet. It's not an aptitude that's defined in any academic spheres where I'm from, but I'll have to trust your opinion for now. Where do we go from here?"

Of course her father would be the one with the more action-oriented response, and Kalina knew exactly the outcome of the situation. Although it bothered her that he was worried she was engaged in illegal practices, it made sense given the context of her witchy mentor from last year.

"I would say it's necessary that Kalina work under a mentor in order to train her abilities. I have a student who, like Kalina, is very powerful, so he had to start learning to control his abilities when he was far younger. It's actually impressive that Kalina has not only been able to keep her aptitude in check for so long, but has actually been able to keep it a secret. I now suspect that her change into a magically infused environment has sharpened her aptitude, making it more powerful, yet more difficult to control. Tell me, how often do you guys use magic at home?"

Kalina kept herself from rolling her eyes, knowing what her mother's reaction would be.

"We like to have a balanced approach," replied Catherine. "I was raised not to use magic frivolously since it's a special gift. Using magic to do the dishes or sweep the floors, for example, would be like using a flamethrower to light a cigarette."

Dr. Toumi smirked and replied, "I have a similar rule in my house, but the drastic shift from that environment to a school for magi is likely what caused the shock to her system. The atmosphere here is flooded with magical aether, likely intensifying her abilities."

Kalina had never thought about it that way. Of course, she had experienced a heightened sense of her aptitude during her test last year, but all other variables were subtle.

"Now," continued Dr. Toumi, "I think it is vital that Kalina have a mentor, and though I've thrown my hat in the ring, she seems not to be interested."

Kalina glanced at her parents, who looked at her with confusion. She didn't think that Dr. Toumi had meant to throw her under the bus or put her in an awkward situation. However, now that he called her out on her decision, she knew that she would have to give an explanation to her parents.

"Well, why not?" asked her mother. "Dr. Toumi has a psychic aptitude as well and you already have a relationship with him from your counseling sessions."

In a brief moment, Kalina thought she could see what Dr. Toumi often saw: a connection of emotions stemming from each person. Her aptitude had worked similarly before, but never in this flavor. There was a delicate harmony to be kept in the group. Kalina wanted to keep her parents calm and accepting of her decision, so she couldn't be tactless. Dr. Toumi wasn't insulted, just curious - same as her father. Dr. Toumi would know if she lied, so she decided to tell the truth without revealing too much.

"Well, I actually asked Mr. Wells if he wanted to be my mentor since he's mentored Phillip. As we discussed, our aptitudes are related somehow. He said he would think about it, but he never got back to me."

Dr. Toumi analyzed her for a few seconds before answering. "I think that he blames himself for the disappearance of Phillip."

Nervous about her parents' reaction, she quickly turned her head towards them. However, they seemed to be taking the mention of his name reasonably well. All her mother did was hold onto the hand of her father.

"Why's that?" answered Ivan Todorova. "It's not like he's the one who banished him anywhere. Besides, that Dalton is the one who had kidnapped Kalina, not him. What else could he have done?"

Kalina was shocked to see her mother just nodding in agreement instead of bursting into tears, walking away, or getting angry. Perhaps she misjudged her maternal strength.

"Weird things happen in Enchanted Forests just like in any other magical wonder," added Catherine. "I don't know where Phillip is or even if he has the ability to time travel like Kalina says, but I'm sure he'll find his way back to us somehow."

The words, the body language... Everything was connecting for Kalina.

"Oh my gosh, you guys are having counseling sessions!" exclaimed Kalina, who never would have been able to imagine either her father or her mother doing it.

"Why are you so surprised, Kalina?" asked her mother. "You're doing counseling with Dr. Toumi, so we thought we would give it a go as well. Sister Maryam recommended that we turn to a spiritual father, and we've been going to him since the beginning of your semester. By the way, she asks about you, and she says 'hi.'"

"Yes, I think that it can be a helpful thing," said Dr. Toumi. "If your parents are okay with Mr. Wells mentoring you, I'm sure that I could convince him to take you on."

"I have no problem with it," shrugged Ivan. Her mother also nodded her head in agreement.

"Well, great. I think we can end that here for now, and I'll make sure to keep you updated if there are any other accidents. Any questions?"

Everyone seemed to leave the office satisfied, even Kalina, which made her suspect that Dr. Toumi had a hand in that. Since her parents were already in the area, they decided to take her out to Winterburg for the rest of the day.

It was less than a half-hour's drive, and the trip to the magical community almost made it worth having to undergo the parent-teacher conference. It had been almost two years since Kalina had visited the village, which she regarded as a special occasion. As they passed a nearby cul-de-sac, Kalina wondered how many of her teachers lived there - including Miss Haverty.

Fortunately for Mr. Todorova, parking was never an issue, and there was a nice gravel plot with lots of space. Being a closed community for magi, all sorts of enchantments were cast in the open, and to Kalina's surprise, the gravel didn't crunch.

"Hm," remarked Catherine, looking out the window. "They put up new acoustic wards."

"Yes, I see them," replied her husband. "Too complicated for me, though. Still, it's a nice touch."

"Do you need anything for school while we're here, Kalina?" asked Ivan.

Kalina wished she could have said yes. She loved to go shopping at all the stores, but the truth was that she didn't really need anything.

"No, but I'd still like to look around."

"Let's head to lunch first," directed her mother, who was aware that Kalina hadn't eaten anything all day.

It was only early noon, so the family decided to head to Psomira, which offered a lot more options to the magical community than it did to the normie one. Here, one could order all sorts of elixirs and ptisanes, including frostwater and pine ale. Her mother ordered some corn coffee, a classic drink among the American community of magi. The interior of the shop had a mediterranean style, the owners being Greeks, though they went all out in Winterburg with marble statues that were enchanted to quietly move and flow.

It was a refreshing rhythm compared to the mundane monotony of any normie environment, and Kalina wondered why there weren't more communities for magi. As she pondered the question, she noticed an asymmetric element in the corner of the cafe. She often heard adults talk about "seeing magic," and although her aptitude made it easier for her, she still was not used to being able to have the vision. After concentrating hard, she earned a slight foresight of her mother tripping as she brought over the tray. Immediately, Kalina caught it before too much of their food would spill. As she helped her mother lay everything on the table, she noticed a woman and a girl leaving Psomira, which was odd since she hadn't noticed them at first when she walked in. When she turned around to look at the corner that had mesmerized her, Kalina realized that it had returned to normal. Putting two together, she stood up and hastened to the door, but it was too late. The woman and the girl were already gone.

"What was that all about?" asked her father, when she returned to the table.

"I thought I saw someone that I might have known," fibbed Kalina. "But I was mistaken. By the way, do you know a spell for being able to see magic that's being done."

"It depends on the situation," replied Ivan. "Normally, I stick with a simple handscope, but untrained magi sometimes use quartz glass."

"There are other ones you can use, too. Like your father said, it depends on what you're looking for. Physical versus non-physical magic. Are they trying to keep it hidden? Are you a magi-archaeologist?"

Her mother continued in what was a very enlightening conversation for Kalina. Despite the strictness of magical use at home, Catherine was still involved in modern research and advancements in physical magic and was subscribed to *MagiTech Monthly*. Before they left Kalina tried a couple of techniques, aiming for that one corner - nothing came of it, but she was still suspicious of the circumstance. Whether or not she was being more paranoid because of last year's events, she wasn't sure. Nonetheless, it didn't hurt to be too careful.

25

TEACHERS AND RESEARCHERS

The heat of the sun through the window warmed Kalina's back, and the smell of old books permeated the air. The pleasant aroma was so strong that it didn't seem quite natural, and Kalina could swear she caught one of the librarians spraying a scented aerosol one early morning.

"Good morning, Kalina. How are you doing today?" greeted Mr. Wells, who was dressed in tweed today.

Kalina, having developed her aptitude more this semester, felt Mr. Wells' approach, but it was more so as if he let her sense his arrival. She wondered if he were able to block her psychic abilities such as Robert could, or even the prescient element of her aptitude, like Dalton. She tensed up at the dark memories of her former mentor, but reminded herself that Mr. Wells was well vetted.

"I'm doing alright," said Kalina. "Shall we begin?"

"Perfect," responded Mr. Wells with a grin. "Straight to business, did you have any specific questions before we start?"

Kalina knew the general direction this appointment would take, so she came prepared in hopes that Mr. Wells would have answers for her queries.

"Well, I know you mentored my brother," began Kalina, but before she could get any further, Mr. Wells jumped in.

"I don't know where he went. I'm sorry. I wish I knew, but I don't."

"I know, and I also know where he went anyway. That wasn't the question I had for you."

Mr. Wells raised his eyebrows, seemingly shocked by the brusqueness and straightforwardness of Kalina's statement, but she continued.

"I don't know how much Dr. Toumi told you, but our powers are inherently related. It shouldn't be much of a surprise since that's how genetics work. I want to be able to use my aptitude with the ease that Phillip teleports."

"I can help you with that," answered Mr. Wells. "There's a lot of research on remote viewing, even in normie circles. I'll have to look more into prescience, though."

"I have two more questions for you about Phillip. First, how does his ability work? Second, has he ever mentioned a library that he's been to?"

Mr. Wells first response was to look around in the library they were in, but he didn't seem to think that she was talking about *that* library. It was as though he were pondering the weight of her statement.

"The first one I can help you with. Phillip can cut into spacetime. He is able to manipulate these cuts in such a way that he can hollow out a kind of tunnel to where he wants to go," he finally stated. "As for the second question... There are several libraries in existence - both mystical and natural. Some I've been to, and others that I've only ever heard rumors of. Unless you can be more specific, I don't think I can help you."

"Actually, I've been there. It was in my report that I gave to the police last year."

"I never read it, but I remember hearing about some parts. Tell me more."

Kalina swallowed before explaining. "When Phillip and I touched, I was sent to what looked like a large library with every sort of book imaginable. It was strange, though - unearthly. My magic didn't work properly there, and what's stranger is that I had met a Byzantine noble. I'm not one-hundred percent sure of what I experienced, but it was some sort of nexus of space and time while also being void of it. Does that make sense to you?"

Mr. Wells didn't answer for a long time. His pupils dilated to the extent that it made his eyes look black, and Kalina felt cut off from him. She lapsed into her magical vision, and it was as though Mr. Wells was disconnected from the whole environment. Never before had she witnessed anything like this absence, and the blood in her veins froze. He then returned to a normal countenance and spoke as though nothing had occurred.

"I've heard rumors and stories of a place like that, but I've never met anyone that's ever witnessed it. The stories say that it has knowledge to make even a non-magus the most powerful man in the world," he said before dropping to a low murmur. "I recommend that you don't tell anyone else about your trip there. Your powers are enough to make people want to use you. If they think that you can give them access to the collective knowledge of the universe, you *will* become a target for some very very dangerous *folk*."

Kalina sighed, "I'm starting to get tired of people saying this to me."

"I'm serious," asserted Mr. Wells.

"I know, but I think figuring out how to go back to this place is the key for me to find Phillip and bring him home."

"I see," said Mr. Wells. "I don't know if I can help you find it, but I can help you improve your aptitude. We'll start with some diagnostics before moving forward with any specific abilities related to yourself as a visionary. Good?"

Kalina nodded, disappointed that he couldn't give her any answers about the strange library she had visited. However, she did learn something new about Mr. Wells. She didn't know what that new information was, but it solidified her suspicions that something was... unique about him. As she contemplated the matter, he reached into his pocket and took out a coin.

"You want to see how well I predict coin flips," stated Kalina.

"Correct. Now, was it your aptitude that led you to foresee this or did you just guess?" asked Mr. Wells.

"You also brought a bag of marbles and a deck of cards to test my ability to predict random draws," she answered, though she had to push herself a little bit to get the full image beyond herself.

Mr. Wells nodded, clearly impressed. "I'm going to spin this quarter ten times, and you're going to guess heads or tails before it falls."

Kalina watched each time the coin danced around the desk. There were no strings of fate and no mythical vision that led her to the answer. It was pure intuition that guided her to predict the right side of the quarter each time.

"Kalina," began Mr. Wells. "Do you know what the probability that you would make a correct guess for a coin flip ten times in a row would be?"

Remembering some of the mathematics her father had taught her, she answered, "Well, the average person would have a fifty percent likelihood of guessing the first coin flip. So would it be fifty percent multiplied by fifty percent ten times?"

"That's exactly right," agreed Mr. Wells. "Fifty percent is really one-half. You're correct about raising it to the tenth power. As a percentage, that comes out to about 0.2 percent. However, that's just the beginning."

Mr. Wells reached into his backpack and took out a sheet of loose-leaf paper and a pen, handing it to Kalina.

"We're going to do the same exercise, except I want you to write all ten of your predictions before I spin the quarter."

Kalina held the pen in her hand and looked down at the sheet he gave her. She wanted to do well, but was unsure of where to begin. The weight of Mr. Wells' patience and stare started to feel heavy, so she began to write the list of rounds to give herself more time to think. Seeing her hesitation, Mr. Wells reassured her.

"Relax. It's just an experiment. When you were making your predictions before, were you calculating them, or did they come to you by instinct?"

Kalina hadn't told him that yet, but he made an excellent point. Pen in hand, she wrote down her first guesses for all ten flips and handed the paper back to Mr. Wells. Without bothering to look at it, he immediately spun the quarter. Each time, he made a notation on the paper whether or not Kalina got it correct.

Afterwards, Kalina sighed, "I got the first seven right, but then I started messing up."

"You got the last one right," responded Mr. Wells. "Besides, seven in a row is still a remarkable feat. There's less than a one percent chance of that ever happening. Do you know what the purpose of this second experiment was?"

"I think you wanted to determine how my aptitude works in a mechanical sense. That's why you asked about my intuition."

"Exactly!" exclaimed Mr. Wells. "When it comes to visionaries or prescient magi, there are different types of predictive methods. The best analogy I can think of is Mark, who's a navigator. He is able to pick up on various environmental qualities that are too subtle for the normal person to sense - air pressure, slope, temperature, soil. I believe that you used a technique similar to this in the first round. Remember, you only had to guess the coin before it fell, but you were allowed to watch the initial trajectory of it."

Kalina nodded her head slowly in understanding.

"I think you've just explained something that I've been feeling," she stated thougfully. "I often have this sense that there are all these dots that I need to connect. Points in time or space that may seemingly be unconnected, but I'm sure that there's a missing piece."

"But there's something else, too," continued Mr. Wells. "Even though you didn't get all the coin tosses right, the fact that you got seven in a row *before* having any information implies that your aptitude may go beyond even trajectory analysis."

Kalina furrowed her eyebrows in confusion. "But I still would have had data from the first set, no?"

"Not enough to do as well as you did in the second round. Seven out of ten might not sound like a lot, but it is still incredible. Let's try something slightly different."

Once again, Mr. Wells reached into his backpack and took out a calculator.

"This calculator has an app that allows you to generate a random coin flip. We're going to do the same exercise as the first round, but this time, with the calculator."

This time, Kalina got the first six right, but messed up on the seventh. The eighth and ninth were likewise correct, but she got the tenth wrong again.

"Hmm," considered Mr. Wells. "There's still a very low likelihood that someone could randomly guess the first six in a row correctly. How many is that again, Kalina?"

"It's one-half to the sixth power," she responded, but her mind was preoccupied with a vision of a rhythm that seemed to be emanating from the calculator.

"Correct, now-"

"I'm sorry," she interrupted. "I think I want to try the second exercise on the calculator."

"Sure," said Mr. Wells, handing back the pen and paper to Kalina, who immediately wrote down twenty guesses for the random coin game.

Mr. Wells happily obliged each of her guesses, writing a check mark for all twenty. By the end, he sat back in his chair and let out a sigh. Kalina sat in hers, a wave of triumph flooding her body. However, based on Mr. Wells' body language, she knew that feeling was about to be taken away from her.

"I should have seen this," he explained. "Calculators - and computers in general - don't often produce truly random numbers. They use an algorithm called pseudorandom number generation. Don't get me wrong, nobody else could do what you just did. However, these numbers are supposed to be close to random, and I'm not sure how you could have guessed them."

"I felt its rhythm," said Kalina, as though it were obvious.

"Its rhythm?"

"Yes, like it was meant to produce either heads or tails. Like it was on a path and had no other choice."

Kalina couldn't quite put into words how she knew the coin would flip on the calculator, but Mr. Wells was clearly trying his best to understand. For a second, she worried that his eyes would dilate again, but he just stared at her instead.

"I'll have to think more on this."

That's it? thought Kalina, disappointed that her new mentor couldn't make a more in-depth analysis. However, she had almost begged him to be her mentor, and she didn't want that to be taken away from her now.

"I understand," she acquiesced.

Mr. Wells nodded his head. "I think that will be all for today. Next time, we'll use the marbles and the deck of cards, but I think we'll see similar results."

Kalina said goodbye, but remained in the library, staring out the window. *If only I could apply what I've just learned to finding Phillip*. Maura would be there any second, and Kalina had an idea that they would figure it out together.

***

"Did he know anything about the library," whispered Maura while the two worked on their chromatic homework for Magical Theory and Practice.

"Not that he shared with me," replied Kalina, filling out her color theory chart. "He just did the experiment. Although, he did give an explanation on how Phillip's teleportation works. Apparently, Phillip can cut into spacetime and make tunnels to where he wants to go. At least, that's the simplified version of it."

"Well, I don't know of any magic that lets us replicate that process," replied Maura, while drawing her linear color model for school.

"I thought that at first, too," said Kalina. "But what if we find someone who's powerful enough to cut through space without having a teleportation aptitude. Do you think Robert's telekinesis would be enough to rip apart the fabric of the cosmos?"

Maura shook her head, "No, it's not about raw power; if so, we'd have several teleporters throughout history. He'll have to learn how to feel for it - just like how I can *feel* sounds or how inscription comes naturally to Aisling. These cuts and tunnels in space remind me of wormholes. Maybe we can do some research on that?"

Kalina looked down at her tedious busywork and sighed.

"We might as well," she answered, closing her books and putting them away.

The two walked up to the librarian's desk and asked if she knew anything about wormholes.

"Well, the model you're most likely familiar with from science-fiction - the Einstein-Rosen bridge - has been shown to be unstable. It's practically impossible in our universe," explained the elderly librarian. "If you're looking for pleasure reading, I can direct you to several authors. However, if you're looking for alternate models and experiments of teleportation, there are a few papers that our school has published. The dean himself worked on one of them when he was a student."

Slowly, the librarian rose from her seat and led them to a series of file-folders, each having a pattern of geometric engravings that slightly differed. Kalina had seen some of the older students use them before to find books or articles, though she herself preferred to peruse the bookshelves.

The librarian stopped at the sixth one and placed her hand out, palm up.

"Non-fiction. Teleportation. Wormholes. Spacetime. Traveling. Scientific research. Papers. Books. Articles."

Immediately, one of the cabinets popped out, and three slips of paper flew into the librarian's hand. She took a pen out and began writing down in a small notepad which books or articles to retrieve for Maura and Kalina.

"You have to be highly specific," she mentioned casually. "Sometimes you'll get a list of books that have nothing to do with the subject matter in question - or maybe they'll have just one short chapter on it. Don't worry, I'll get you two girls pieces of scientific literature that you'll find easy to understand."

"Can we get Dean Schulz's paper?" requested Maura.

"Of course. Since he and his partner were students when they wrote it, it may be closer to your level. I remember helping those two sweethearts when they were in school. Fond times."

Kalina and Maura snapped their heads at each other grinning about the librarian's comment on the dean. *What did the librarian mean by "sweethearts?"*

"Their research advisor was Mr. Smith," she continued while waving the file notecards back into their spots. "I believe he's going to retire next year. If you have any questions, you may want to ask him before he leaves campus for the day."

The librarian led them back to her desk and speedily typed out the note into the system.

"I'll have you two start out with a book on the fundamentals of theoretical physics, and the research paper will be printed out. Follow the light."

Kalina had seen the cracks in the wooden floorboards glow before, especially when there were several students studying in the library. Neither of the two students knew how the magic worked, but some talented magus had come up with an algorithm that led people to the exact book they were looking for.

"A bit of a step up from the Dewey Decimal System," stated Maura. "I wonder how they engineered it."

"The algorithm itself should be simple: use Dewey's numbers as a location - like GPS coordinates, and then produce a path to the book," guessed Kalina, who stopped at the shelf their book was on. It took a second for her to trace the light to the book, but it was much faster than having to speed read several digits at a time.

When they returned to the librarian's desk to check out *From Newton to Mandelbrot*, they found Dean Schulz's academic paper waiting for them.

"Happy reading," said the librarian, while scanning the book.

Maura took the paper, and as they were leaving the library, she started to read it.

"Out of curiosity, Kalina, what's your mother's maiden name?"

"Nelson," she answered. "I'm actually distantly related to Robert. Why?"

Maura handed the paper to Kalina, who immediately stopped in her tracks. *An Experiment on Traveling for Non-Aptitude Magi* by John Schulz and Catherine Nelson.

"When she said they were sweethearts, she probably just meant that they were good kids right?" asked Kalina.

"We could always ask Mr. Smith," suggested Maura, clearly playing the side of tact at the moment.

Kalina had never felt so much shock in her life. Her stomach dropped, and her heart started racing. The hallway spun around her.

"They were just sweet kids when they were in school, right," she muttered.

"Why don't we get some food Kalina. We don't want to miss dinner, and we've already done enough studying today."

26

CATCHING THE NEWS

Kalina and Maura both rushed out of their last class in order to find Mr. Smith, the alchemy teacher, before he left the campus for the weekend. They had already missed him the day before, and the two wanted to make sure they got a chance to talk to him before he left for the weekend.

"Are you sure he'll come this way and not through the science hall?" asked Maura anxiously.

"The teacher's lounge is by this stairwell," reassured Kalina, who was certain by use of her prescience. "I'm absolutely certain he takes a break before leaving at the end of the school day."

As soon as she said those words, the old teacher had pushed open the double doors that led to the staircase.

"Mr. Smith!" exclaimed Maura, excitedly. "May we ask you a few questions, please?"

Mr. Smith gave them a quizzical regard before saying, "You two aren't in my class. Shouldn't you be asking Mrs. Blackwell to help you?"

"It's an extracurricular matter," replied Kalina. "We were hoping you could explain to us a little bit about the research paper my mom and Dean Schulz did under your supervision."

"Oh, sure," replied Mr. Smith with a nostalgic twinkle in his eye. "It's been a couple of decades, though. I believe their research was about quantum teleportation, yes? They were two very talented students. I don't think I've seen another ambitious set walk through my classroom since then. I always thought it serendipitous that your brother turned out to have a teleportation aptitude, but you have a different one don't you?"

"I do," responded Kalina evasively. "Do you think their research may have influenced my brother's aptitude?"

"Perhaps it may have affected your mother's genetics, but I'm not a biologist. That is a question that is really best directed towards Mrs. Blackwell. As for that specific research paper... Well, like I said, it's been a couple of decades since I've looked at it, so I can't tell you more than what's written on ink, which I assume you have. However, I believe that they discovered that there are minute instances of slivers of rips in the fabric of space that are constantly yet randomly occurring. They were able to accurately predict one of those instances and passed an electron through that rip. It was that research paper that got Dean Schulz a scholarship for University of New Amsterdam. I even remember the VBM being interested in their work, but I don't think the research has gone further than what they did. Research costs a lot of money, you know."

"Wow," said Maura. "That's a lot of information. Thank you so much."

"Well, if you girls don't have anything else to ask me, my weekend is just about to begin -"

"I do have one more question," stated Kalina, her heart racing. She could barely get her next sentence out without stuttering. "D-dean Schulz and my... my mom... what was their umm relationship like?"

The query did not seem to catch Mr. Smith off guard, as Kalina expected it might. However, at his age, this teacher must have seen and been asked almost every question there is under the sun.

"Well, Kalina, I won't lie to you, and if you must know, they were high school sweethearts. I believe they broke up after they graduated. They had different futures envisioned for themselves. That being said, I wouldn't dwell on it. Now, have a good evening."

"You, too, Mr. Smith," said Maura, who placed a hand on Kalina's shoulder.

Of course, Kalina knew deep down what the story was going to be, and of course, it didn't matter. It's not like Dean Schulz was her father. Nonetheless, she was left as speechless as a fish in water.

"Are you okay," checked Maura, clearly worried about her friend. She herself couldn't see what the big deal was, aware that her own parents saw other people before they had met each other. To be fair, it wasn't like one of those people was one of her teachers.

Kalina nodded her head, and changed the subject . "Let's go find Robert. I want his opinion on what we've discovered. He'll be coming from the weightroom right about now."

Kalina and Maura silently walked down the hallway, which had quieted down significantly since classes were over. Their Cardinal

Key dress shoes tapped on the marble tiles. Right enough, Robert was exiting the gym with a bottle of frostwater in hand.

"Well, how are you, Kalina?" he greeted.

"Not too bad," she replied. "We've got some information that we'd like to discuss. Apparently there's a research paper from a couple of decades ago."

"Sounds great," said Robert. "You know, I was speaking to Aisling earlier, and she said she and Mark wanted to meet up at the mess hall, and she asked me to tell you. Clearly she has something to show us. Do you mind waiting until dinner to share?"

"No, not at all."

"Great, I'll see you then."

Robert exited the building and jogged off towards the boys' dormitory, leaving Maura and Kalina behind.

"How come he didn't say 'hi' to me?" asked Maura. "Kind of rude, no?"

"I don't think he meant anything by it," comforted Kalina. "Did you see the sweat on him? I know when I have an intense workout, it takes a little time for my brain cells to recharge."

"Fair enough," sighed Maura, who put a hundred and ten percent into hockey and stoickee. "Well, dinner won't be for at least another hour. We might as well get some studying done back at the dorm."

Kalina agreed and the pair of them returned to the girls' dormitory. After greeting Mrs. Donna, they headed upstairs and promptly decided that since they had all weekend to work, they might as well take a break and play some magic Uno.

"It's kind of like studying color theory," justified Maura, to which Kalina couldn't help but agree.

After an intense round, where the two girls had elevated the game to colors outside of the visible spectrum , Kalina checked her phone to find that Robert had already texted her.

"Looks like it's time for dinner," she informed Maura, and the two hungry students eagerly hurried to the mess hall.

After picking their food, it wasn't hard for them to find Robert, Aisling, and Mark. The three were all staring at an old Cardinal Key yearbook.

"Where'd you get that from?" asked Maura as she took a seat next to her sister. Aisling was well aware that she couldn't keep her sister out of the conversation since she was Kalina's roommate, but she was still anxious about involving her. "It's definitely older than mom's."

"It's from the library," responded Aisling in an annoyed tone. "I've checked it out before - last year, remember?"

Maura rolled her eyes - as if she were supposed to recall everything that her sister had ever done. This, however, was an instance that Maura remembered vividly.

"The summer you were going on and on about the missing students of '69. How could anyone forget," said Maura sarcastically

Aisling glared at her sister before continuing, "Well, there's an interesting description of a new student who was a junior who played on the Elementafl team. A student named 'Philip.' I had never put two and two together, but maybe this is where our Phillip could have gone."

Kalina sat upright when she heard the name. Could Aisling have found undeniable proof that her brother had in fact time-traveled. She took the yearbook that Aisling handed her and studied it intensely. Although she was sure this *could* be him, she didn't want to get her hopes up for what could also be nothing.

"Well," began Kalina, eyeing the aged book. She carefully examined the fragile yellow pages in the hopes of finding any more hints. "It *could* be him. He would be a junior, but there's no picture of him, and they don't have his last name. They even spelt his first name differently. He has two *l*'s not one."

"What are the odds, though?" pushed Aisling. "I mean, there's a mysterious 'Philip' who appears out of nowhere in 1969. I checked the yearbooks afterwards and beforehand, and he's not mentioned. In fact, there are no other Philip's or Phillip's at all! This has to be him."

Kalina sighed, trying to focus, but she *did* believe Aisling's theory - it matched with her own after all. Nonetheless, she preferred her evidence to be rigorous and not speculative.

"Either way," she responded, pushing the yearbook back to Aisling. "We still need a plan to get to him, and I think Maura and I have found something very interesting."

The girls' hadn't brought the article with them since they didn't want it to get stained at dinner. However, they were still able to give the gist of it to the rest of the group.

"Robert, I was wondering if you might be able to use telekinesis to make a rip in the fabric of space," said Kalina.

"I'm afraid it's not in the physical nature of telekinesis," he responded, cutting into his chicken breast. "Do you realize how many telekinetics there are? Even you guys can move objects around with an incantation. Sure I'm powerful, but someone before me would have definitely found a way to rip open the fabric of space if it were possible. Sorry, I don't mean to shut you down by being blunt."

"What if you didn't need to actually rip open space itself," considered Maura. "The article states that there may already be these cuts in the fabric of space, appearing at seemingly random intervals of time and space. Assuming that we could catch one of these miniscule rips, it may be possible to stabilize its place and expand the already present rip. Maybe if you could *feel* it, Robert, you would know what to do?"

"I suppose I could give it a try, but that's still assuming we find one of these rips. How complex are the techniques in your research paper?"

"Hold on," interrupted Mark. "Say we get all of this done and we use this rip in the fabric of space, how do we know where we'll end up? Where do you even plan on ending up?"

Kalina swallowed a bite of her roasted broccoli before answering. "Remember that library I mentioned? I think that's the best case scenario of where we'll end up."

"And do you have a plan on getting there?" pressured Mark.

"Isn't that what we're working on right now?" retorted Kalina, who didn't like the subtle aggressiveness of Mark's interrogation. "You're a navigator after all."

"Okay, fine. I'll play ball. Tell me where your library is, and I'll get you there," challenged Mark.

Kalina hesitated, frustrated at both her lack of understanding as well as the attitude Mark was giving her. He never would have acted this way had Phillip been present. Robert gave her a sympathetic look, but he knew perhaps less than she did.

"Give me a moment to think," requested Kalina, calming herself down. She closed her eyes, thinking about what she recalled. "I entered the mysterious library right after I made contact with Phillip on the edge of where the enchanted forest met Ms. Dalton's private residence. I know it was the border because of where the tree stood and the abrupt change in the weather. I was suddenly transported to this Library, but when I left it, over a month had passed and you all were on spring break. I arrived back in the enchanted forest, but don't ask how I made my way back to campus. I still don't know how that worked. I don't think the library is in our world. My best guess is that it's some sort of nexus of space and time."

Nobody was eating their dinner while she spoke. Instead they were focused on taking in her words carefully, and even Mark seemed to have softened up. Aisling picked at her food with her fork, clearly struggling to come up with a theory.

Robert took a sip of water before he began, saying "What you're describing sounds like a place that's not psychological, since you were there in material form. I wonder if it exists outside of what we recognize as a... 'travelable' (is that a word?) location. Meaning, if we were to teleport there, like you suggest, we would have to make sure that one end of the portal is closed off from the rest of our dimension."

"So we'd be going nowhere - literally," scoffed Mark. Although she knew Mark had a chip on his shoulder against Robert, she had to admit that what he just said did sound like nonsense. Mark himself cut off a large chunk of his chicken and bit down on it while giving Robert an incredulous look.

"Actually, that could make sense," said Aisling, and all eyes turned to her. "You see, I recall learning back in my geometry class about different surfaces and their topological qualities. The math is above me, but if Phillip figured out how to teleport without puncturing into space that's topologically connected to our reality, then maybe that's where your library could be, and that's why it would look like there's nothing on the other side. Again, I don't know a lot about this kind of stuff. It's just an idea."

Mark looked like he wanted to agree with his girlfriend, but he remained scrupulously critical.

"Do we even know if Phillip ever visited this library? We could be going somewhere he's never actually been before. How do we know that it wasn't *your* aptitude that led you there?"

He tried to be as courteous as he could this time, but Kalina was still annoyed by the constant holes in their working theories. Again, Robert came to her aid having just swallowed some butternut squash.

"I have a working theory about that," he countered, and eyed their surroundings. "I'm wondering if there was something - *a cer-*

tain kind of spell - that might have mixed or amplified Kalina's and Phillip's aptitudes."

The way Robert said it silenced everyone at the table, and Kalina immediately realized that it was the blood magic ritual that the three had used in order to find and rescue her. It made perfect sense why she would have traveled across time and into some quasi-intellectual realm with the help of Phillip. As a conjecture, it could also explain why it allowed Phillip to travel across the temporal element of space-time.

The only person who did not understand what everyone was thinking was Maura, who leaned into Kalina's ear and muttered, "What's he talking about?"

"I'll tell you later," responded Kalina. "We can't talk about it in the mess hall."

Even Mark nodded his head slowly.

"You know what? I think we've actually got a lot of information to work with, and no doubt your research papers will tell us more," he acquiesced - that or he was getting tired of the conversation. "In any case, I'm full, and I have homework to work on."

He put his plate in the dispenser and left without Aisling, who said goodnight to him. It didn't take long for the rest of the group to disband, and Kalina headed back to her dorm with a mixture of hope and pessimism.

27
FRIENDS AND FORECASTING

"You guys have no idea how stressed I am," announced Olympia, who gestured with a club sandwich in hand . "I knew that seventh grade was going to be a lot tougher, but I don't think I was prepared for all the homework and exams we were getting. If I don't get straight A's, my parents are going to be miffed!"

"Tell me about it," replied Maura sarcastically. For a moment, Kalina was reminded of her glimpse into Maura's home life.

"I'd rather not," retorted Olympia, who was locked in and serious. It wasn't for nothing that she maintained a reputation for being a somewhat neurotic high-achiever. "I hope we're still on for our study session later today. Is Alice coming?"

"She said she would be," answered Kalina. "I wonder if she would invite Laurelle. We haven't heard much more about her from Alice since our last conversation. Did she ever tell any teachers?"

"She talked to me," began Maura, as the three stood on the path between the dorms and the main building. "I didn't say anything because you were focused on other matters, but Alice told me that the last time she checked, the room had been cleaned up. Laurelle has even started acting friendlier to her. Well, cordial at the least. This was around the same time as you had your seizure."

"Do you think we should invite her then?" suggested Kalina, hoping to bring her old roommate back into the thick of their friendship.

Maura shrugged and shuffled her feet before responding, "Well, I'm always open to giving my friends the benefit of the doubt."

Olympia sighed, "I didn't witness most of this. I say that since it's Alice's roommate, we should let her decide."

"I'll text her right now," said Maura, who decided that was a fair answer.

"Well, I have to go meet Mr. Wells in the library right now, but I'll meet up with you all afterwards."

"Hold on, Kalina," interrupted Maura before Kalina left. "It looks like it may rain, so we may not be studying on the lawn. We'll try to find an empty classroom, but if we can't, I'll text you where we are."

"Sounds good!" exclaimed Kalina before hurrying off to find Mr. Wells.

By the time she got to the library, she knew that he would be there waiting for her. It was unusual for him to arrive earlier, but she had gotten caught up talking to Olympia and Maura. She promptly apologized, but he reassured her that it was okay.

"How has your practice with the cards been going?" he started.

A couple weeks ago, he had given her a deck of cards and asked her to practice predicting the sequence of a shuffle. He had advised her to start off with predicting the colors, then the suits, then the numbers, and then eventually both at the same time. Although it seemed like a mundane and almost useless task, Kalina had obliged her mentor. She wondered if mastering the unimportant stuff first would help improve her precognitive visions.

"I'm able to get all the colors and suits, but the highest streak I've gotten with the numbers is forty-two cards," responded Kalina, shaking her head. She wished to be perfect, but she still fell short. "The last time I tried predicting both suits and numbers, I ended up getting only twenty-two in a row."

"That's still enough to get you kicked out of Las Vegas," joked Mr. Wells. "But I can see you've been working very hard on it. Do you mind demonstrating to me how far you've gotten."

Kalina took out the cards he had given her and gave them a quick shuffle. This time, she had accurately predicted the thirty-seven in a row. Mr. Wells nodded his head in approval and whispered something in a melodic foreign language. When he waved his fingers, the deck of cards put themselves together back in their deck and then neatly tucked away inside his backpack. For the first time, Kalina noticed the difference in his magical casting. It certainly wasn't an American style, nor was it the slavic style that she witnessed from her dad. The movements of his hands while he incanted was fluid - more organic and natural, causing her to wonder if he was homeschooled.

"Excellent," he commended, while jotting down a note. "I suspect that when you're faced with highly complex forms of randomness, it's harder for you to use your aptitude. I won't force you to keep practicing, though. I can imagine how tedious you find it. I do want to move on to a different technique for the time being. I think I mentioned some research into remote viewing. Do you have any experience with that?"

"Only a little," confessed Kalina. "And I was advised against the techniques I was using to induce it."

Mr. Wells raised an eyebrow, analyzing the weight of her statement.

"I see," he said, even though Kalina didn't mention any specifics. "We won't be using binaural beats or any external factors to force it out of you. If our hypothesis that your aptitude patterns after your brother's is correct, then we may be able to map out where in the world you can see using navigation techniques - kind of like setting up a video chat somewhere else."

"Would I be able to use it to see different points in time as well?" she asked, aware that it was the specialty of her aptitude. She would just have to trust that Mr. Wells knew what he was talking about.

"I'm not sure how that would translate, but for now, let's focus on getting you to a specific place," said Mr. Wells, who had taken out a binder from his backpack. Kalina was sure that if there were more information about precognition, then he would have found it. However, it was a tricky domain of magic that still holds a negative connotation among many magi, including her own father. "Here's a place that I'm sure you know well."

"If this is based on your curriculum for Phillip, then I'm guessing it's my address."

She opened the binder and was proven right.

"Take a second to look at the cartographical analysis of where your home is, and try to look into it."

Kalina focused intensely on the papers before her. Although the principles behind navigation were mostly self-explanatory, she couldn't just pop herself into her house like Phillip was prone to do.

"Are you trying to squeeze yourself there?" teased Mr. Wells. "Your face is as red as a tomato."

Remaining silent, Kalina looked up at him and knew he was right. She relaxed each of her muscles and let go of the picture of her home. She had to *understand* where it was. No, she had to *experience* it. Her eyes closed, and she felt much lighter.

There was no floating sensation, which she had felt under the tutelage of Dalton or while listening to binaural beats. She was simply *there*. Except, when she opened her eyes, all she saw was a dense wetland. There were no houses, no people, but a few animals that she caught glimpses of. Eventually, her confusion overtook her, and she found herself sitting across Mr. Wells in the library again.

"Well?" he prompted.

"I don't think I ended up there. All I saw was an uninhabited wetland. Can I try again?"

Mr. Wells shrugged and leaned back in his seat. "Go for it."

This time, Kalina reminded herself of where home was. How she got there from Cardinal Key, what it looked like, and where it was on the map. Then, she cleared her mind and repeated the process. This time, when she opened her eyes, she found herself in another wetland. *That looks like the same tree that I saw last time*, she noted, and then the rest of the scene fell into place. Realizing she had failed once again, she pulled herself back into her corporeal body.

"Same thing," she said tersely before Mr. Wells could get a word in.

"I have a suspicion," explained Mr. Wells. "I think you got the place correct. Perhaps you haven't gotten the right time. If you did see an uninhabited marsh, then you might have actually witnessed Virginia before it was discovered and inhabited by European settlers."

"Well that's random," gasped Kalina in frustration. "Why did I see *that* and not the present or the future? And why that time period?"

"That may be a question I'll have to reflect on. I'll leave you to practice this method and play around with it - *within reason*, of course."

Kalina caught the accusation in his tone. If she hadn't already played around with advanced - *dangerous* - forms of magic, she would have blamed him for it. Still, he knew how to turn what was once an exciting adventure into a dull exercise in math and trigonometry.

"Got it," affirmed Kalina. "Do you want your binder back?"

"No," he said, zipping up his backpack. "You're my student now, and you should use it to practice. I'll see you next week."

"Before you go, I have a couple questions," requested Kalina.

"Go ahead."

"A few weeks ago, we briefly talked about Phillip's aptitude. I've been doing more research, and I was confused on a couple of points.

First of all, how can Phillip just puncture through space and end up somewhere?"

"That requires a bit of advanced mathematics, but the best theory modern theoretical physicists have is that teleporters can make a topological cut - a small tear that quickly collapses - through space-time into a higher dimensional fabric. There, points that are distant in our universe can briefly be made adjacent. It's not as though he's conscious that that's what he's doing - if the theory is true at all.

"As to your library question - it's possible for him to go to another world. If it's not something that exists in the cosmos, that's another story. I suppose he could make an orthogonal leap into a higher dimension that's disconnected from ours, but I'm not entirely sure."

"You're right, that does require advanced mathematics," huffed Kalina, who only understood about fifty percent of what Mr. Wells had just explained. Even then, it was only based off the brief hypothesis that Aisling herself gave. In any case, it seemed that Mr. Wells needed to go, so she didn't ask for any more explanation.

Kalina thanked him, and then tucked it away in her own backpack. It was a shorter session than usual, but she was glad because she needed to find Maura and her friends for studying. The pitter-patter against the library window had informed Kalina that it was raining, and she checked her phone for Maura's text.

It started raining once we got outside. I'll let you know where we go.

All the classrooms are locked, so I offered our dormitory.

Laurelle has decided to join us.

Kalina wasn't sure whether or not she was pleased about Laurelle joining a study session in her personal space. She trusted Maura and the other girls, and she certainly didn't have anything to hide. *You do get butterflies and anxiety often after using your aptitude. It's probably nothing*, she reassured herself. Figuring that a rainy fall evening called for some hot cocoa, Kalina stopped at the mess hall and picked up five cups. She carried four in a carrier, and one for herself, but when she got to the door, she realized that she was one hand short for her umbrella. Fortunately, Mrs. Donna was at the right place at the right time and had seen her struggling.

"Do you need some help, honey?" she offered, to which Kalina nodded. The middle-aged woman held a cup of coffee in one hand and an umbrella in the other. After pushing the door open, she said to Kalina, "Here's a spell you'll want to remember for the future: *coprimi, parapluie*!"

Her umbrella popped out and was large enough to cover the two of them as they walked towards the girls' dormitory. Mrs. Donna let go of the umbrella which continued to hover over them as they walked.

"Was that French?" asked Kalina.

"The last part," confirmed Mrs. Donna. "'Comprimi' is Italian for 'cover me.' You can sometimes mix languages when you are incanting, you know."

"Nobody told me that," replied Kalina. "Why do people prefer to use foreign languages over English so often? I know that it has the benefit of widening your range and hiding your spells from other magi, but you'd think on average, people would tend to use English here."

"It's a bulky language, that's why," explained Mrs. Donna. "We teach languages like Latin and Greek because they rhyme easily. Some people do use English a lot, but it's not as easy for me. If you'll notice, there are seven syllables in my spell. A very magical number indeed."

"Could you repeat it?" requested Kalina, trying not to get her shoes wet in the puddles.

This time, Mrs. Donna stated the incantation plainly, "Comprimi parapluie. Cover me, umbrella. I'm sure you know by now that it's better to cast spells that are specific - the more specific, the better."

"Yes," responded Kalina. "Doesn't your spell have the added benefit of appealing to the nature of the umbrella?"

"Very good!" exclaimed Mrs. Donna. "Though, to be honest, I never really understood how something could be appealing to an inanimate object. I suppose it's just a figure of speech."

The two had finally arrived at the girls' dormitory, and since Kalina's hands were full, Mrs. Donna offered to check her in.

"I already know that you have a lot of studying on your plate. It's a shame the weather has to beat you down, too."

Kalina thanked Mrs. Donna, and headed over to the leverate, commanding it to take her to the sixth floor. Even though her dorm room was closed, Kalina could hear the voices of her four friends carry down the hall. *Stephanie might come in and ask us to quiet down*, she thought. Instead of fumbling with her materials, Kalina kicked the bottom of the door to let them open it for her.

"Oh!" exclaimed Maura. "It's you. I thought it was Stephanie coming to tell us to quiet down again. What have you got?"

"It's a cool, rainy day, so I thought I would get us some hot chocolates for studying!"

"Thank you so much!" said Alice, and each girl took her own.

Kalina noted when Laurelle took her own hot chocolate and said thank you. Nothing seemed off, but Kalina still had those butterflies in her stomach.

The quintet of students put their heads down and continued studying for biology. Mrs. Blackwell was a notoriously harsh grader, but fortunately Olympia had a knack for the natural sciences. Kalina struggled to understand why certain plants had magical properties, but that was more likely a question to be brought up in Magical Theory.

"Do you see review question eleven?" began Maura, frustrated. "Suppose an incense were to be made in order to induce stimulation. Which herbs and which of their parts should be processed in order to make this bundle?"

"That's easy," began Laurelle, who explained the differences between leaves, stems, roots, and flowers with respect to their properties. Kalina glanced at Olympia and realized that she wasn't the only one who noticed that the girl who was interested in wicca knew all about incense. Of course, there were a variety of ways to use incense - both for magical and non-magical purposes. That didn't mean it had a prestigious reputation among the magical community.

After about an hour of going over the plant kingdom, Olympia gave a tired sigh and said, "I'm ready to go to the mess hall for dinner."

"I'll go with you," joined Alice quickly, looking at Maura and Kalina.

Kalina just shrugged and said, "The hot chocolate was heavy, and I've been snacking a lot recently. I think I'll skip dinner tonight and have a little extra at breakfast tomorrow morning."

In solidarity, Maura stated that she would do the same, but Laurelle said that she wanted to do some more studying in her own dorm for her art class. Once the girls left, Kalina was finally free to talk to Maura about her session with Mr. Wells.

"Did you find out why you ended up seeing only that point in history?" she asked.

"No," answered Kalina. "But to be honest, I can't shrug off the odd nature of Mr. Wells. I know he teaches science, but his movements are so *unscientific*."

"He could just be homeschooled like he said," countered Maura, who tied up their full trash bag and placed it by their door to take out tomorrow morning.

"That's what I thought. I did tell you about his eyes turning black, didn't I?"

"You did," confirmed Maura. "I asked my sister about it, but she said that she's never seen that happen to him before. I'm guessing you want to find him in the collective subconsciousness?"

Kalina didn't wait for Maura to change her mind, and the roommates got to work. It didn't take them nearly as long as it did the first time, and Kalina reached her personal library almost immediately. Based on her previous visits, she stuck to the first shelf before the front desk. She and Mr. Wells saw each other regularly now, which made him part of her personal orbit. Towards the bottom, a thick, hard, leatherbound codex caught her attention.

The tome was significantly heavier than any other book she had perused from the shelves. It even had a lock on the side, preventing her from opening it. *That's odd*, she considered. *Normally, the key is a type of encryption.* After noting the impenetrable clasp, she took a closer look at the title. The letters, large and warped, were engraved onto the leather and gilded. An advanced celtic interlace framed the cover, twisting into wolves that guarded each corner. *Aisling would love to analyze the gaelic inscription*, thought Kalina. For now, the best she could do was copy down the title - meant to be the name of the person. After writing and rewriting it, she stared at letters once more, aiming to memorize them in order to show them to Maura. Once she was confident she could copy the inscription by heart, she pulled back into the physical plane.

"Did you find him?" asked Maura without missing a beat, but Kalina needed a second to readjust. When she looked at the clock, she saw that she had been gone for the same amount of time that she had spent in the collective subconsciousness, meaning that she didn't abuse her magic.

"I don't know," she finally stated. "I did find this strange book with a strange cover."

Before she could forget, she rushed to her desk and wrote down the letters *PAPBBHID* and presented them to Maura while describing what the book looked like.

"It's not Aisling's is it?" checked Maura.

"Definitely not," asserted Kalina. "I've never seen another book like this."

"And the letter design... let me copy it down."

Kalina watched as Maura rewrote the script so that it matched the style of the book.

"Yes!" exclaimed Kalina. "That's exactly how they were painted!"

"It's called uncial," explained Maura. "It's the old style of writing in Irish. Are you sure it's not Aisling or even me? I can't think of anyone at this school who's more Irish than us. Unless you know someone?"

Kalina shook her head and responded, "I really do *feel* like this is Mr. Wells' book. He's just so mysterious. I might just need to head to bed and ask Robert for help tomorrow or another day."

Maura agreed, turned off the lights, and headed straight to bed. As Kalina drifted off, she caught on to a familiar dream. This time, in slow motion, Mr. Wells started to emerge from the ground. Just as he was about to fully come out, he began to decrease in size, becoming younger, until he was a baby and sunk back into the earth.

28

PLOTS AND PLANS

"I need this break so badly," claimed Maura, who had just entered their dorm. She was thoroughly drenched from field hockey practice in the rain. "By the way, my sister wanted to meet tomorrow morning for breakfast before we all left for Thanksgiving."

"Sounds like a plan," confirmed Kalina. "By the way, Robert finally reached back to me."

"It's been over a week," stated Maura. "But I suppose he has a lot on his plate with classes, too."

"That was the reason he gave," replied Kalina. "He wants to meet in the collective subconsciousness after dinner, around eight tonight. It's 6:30 now. Do you think you can hum me in?"

"Oh, alright. Let me take a shower first - I'm freezing! Then we can get ourselves to the mess hall."

"Don't take too long!" demanded Kalina, as Maura closed the door behind her.

Fortunately for Kalina, Maura was famished, and she had no desire to take as much time as she normally did. The duo grabbed their brown rain boots and Cardinal crimson umbrellas before tromping down to dinner.

"I'm sick of the rain. Isn't there some kind of incantation that can keep us dry?" complained Kalina.

"Well, if you read the seventh grade handbook..." teased Maura.

"Is there actually one in there?" asked Kalina, seriously.

"No, but the fact that you still haven't read it astonishes me. Your pleats would look a lot neater if you would use the recipe in there instead of ironing them by hand."

"You know my family is weird about using magic for chores," justified Kalina, who in truth had just been too lazy and forgetful to read the guide. "They say it's a listless and profane use of magic."

"My grandmother said something similar to me once, but she doesn't really follow that tradition anymore."

The two girls spent a great deal of time picking and choosing from the Thanksgiving platter set out for students before the holiday: roast turkey, smoked salmon, casseroles of various assortments, grilled vegetables, and a variety of pies and pastries that left them defeated at their seats.

"I don't know if I'll be able to enter the collective subconsciousness like this," groaned Kalina as they walked back to the girls' dormitory. "It makes the mind sleepy, but maybe that will help."

"Oh, just walk it off," replied Maura jovially.

"How are you so giddy?" questioned Kalina. "You ate nearly twice as much as me!"

"Well, I did go to field hockey before this, plus I've been saving myself all day for tonight's dinner. I didn't get to try everything last year, so I made it a goal to try a little bit of each dish this year," she stated triumphantly.

"The staff and students really did outdo themselves, didn't they?" agreed Kalina, who felt as though her stomach were about to pop.

Once the two returned to their dorm, they took a few minutes to rest before beginning the ritual. Before they began, however, Maura made a grave request.

"I'm wondering if you could take a peek inside Laurelle's subconscious," she suggested. "I'm getting a strange feeling from her. I also don't think you should tell Robert about it. He seems hesitant to dig into other people's minds."

"You're right. I've been getting some weird vibes from her. I thought it was just me," replied Kalina. "And don't worry, I won't tell Robert, but I think it will be better if I do our mission afterwards. I want to make sure he doesn't catch me intruding in on Laurelle."

"That makes sense. Take your time," replied Maura, who promptly performed her harmony.

Kalina had been getting more and more efficient about slipping into the realm of the intellect, and in no time, she found herself amidst her orderly library, brighter and sharper than it had been in the past. Almost immediately, she felt a knocking at the entrance. Sensing that it was Robert, she unlocked the doors and let him in.

"You're getting stronger," he remarked as he strode into her own mental space. "I'm not sure I could have broken down your doors."

"Thank you," responded Kalina, who couldn't help but feel pleased with herself. "You got my text about Mr. Wells?"

"Yes, I did. I don't normally like poking around people's personal lives, but you do have me intrigued. Can I see the book?"

"Yes, of course," answered Kalina, turning around to begin her search for it. "It should be around here somewhere."

Kalina first scanned the desk, where she remembered books of importance taking place. Not only was she now mentored by Mr. Wells, but she had a keen interest in his background. Unfortunately the book wasn't there, and Robert followed her as she started examining the bookshelves. When she reached a section that seemed totally foreign to her personal relationships, she double checked each book individually. Thankfully, Robert was patient, but she still couldn't find the Insular codex from last time.

"People can't just disappear, can they?" asked Kalina.

"It's never happened to me. Maybe we should try looking for his locker. Well... a door in your head," he suggested.

The two exited the library and entered the hallway. Kalina could vaguely tell whose door they were passing. Maura, her mother, her father - Phillip's wasn't there at the moment, but that didn't mean he wasn't in the hallway at all. It could also mean that he was exceptionally distant. Eventually, they came to a door that was grossly inverted and backwards. Though the others were unique in design, they were thematic to the architecture of Kalina's mental space - wooden and uniform in dimension. The door before her was not; it was obsidian black carved out of a material Kalina could not discern. There was a thick sunken metal frame around the door, giving it the odd look of being simultaneously bloated and abyssal. Had Kalina been before it on the earthly plane, she would have turned away from whatever ghastly building decided to use it to welcome its visitors.

"I've never seen anything like this before," said Robert in disgust. "It doesn't belong here."

"You're not seeing this as a locker?" questioned Kalina.

"No, I see the doors, nor have I ever seen a locker that looked like this. That's Mr. Wells' alright, but it's totally backwards and... almost inhuman."

"Shall we enter?"

"No!" exclaimed Robert, causing Kalina to startle. "Sorry, but one thing you'll learn is to not mess around in the psychic plane. There's a reason why we stick to our own mental maps and don't go out into the wild. There's always a bigger fish out there, and granted that were mortals, that's basically every nonhuman entity that we come across. Come, let's go to my place."

Robert turned away, and his door was serendipitously opposite to them, causing Kalina to wonder if it was happenstance or by his will that it was placed there. He opened his door, leading her into what looked like a copy of the Cardinal Key main building.

"What happened to the football field and the locker room?"

"I've had to expand, especially since football is no longer my main identity," he explained.

"You mean you could just change your mental landscape?" wondered Kalina, who was thinking about what she could do in her mind.

"Not manually, that takes a lot of tedious work. Plus that's not my aptitude. Let's say it was more of a change in sentiment and ability. Come on," directed Robert. "There should be lockers down the hallway."

Kalina's eyes widened at the structured array of lockers before them. Unlike the chaotic labyrinth she previously witnessed, this one was patterned and gridlike. Instead of the plain steel gray, they were all now crimson with etched bronze designs.

"That's mine!" she recognized, as they passed the first set. Hers had a winding array of flowering dogwood branches that acted as a border. "They don't have locks anymore."

"That doesn't mean it's easy for me to open them up," he stated as he continued walking.

Kalina followed contently, taking in everything she could of her surroundings. She recognized more than a few people that Robert had connections to, but when he stopped in his tracks , she almost bumped into him. She turned towards his gaze, but there was only a blank patch of wall. It took her a moment to realize that there should have been another red locker in its place.

"Do you think this is where Mr. Wells is supposed to be?" asked Kalina, hoping that he could give her more answers than questions.

"It should not be possible. Even the most talented telepaths and psychics leave an imprint of their consciousness. I'll see if there is a way I can ask Dr. Toumi about it. I know he and Mr. Wells are friends, but I don't want another situation like Dalton's to happen again. You didn't see any lockers saying Henry Wells on them did you?"

Kalina shook her head as she examined her surroundings. She was in awe of how clean Robert's psychic space appeared to her.

"No, but I wonder why he appeared in your hallway but not in mine," continued Robert.

Kalina had her own theory about her ability to sense supernatural phenomena, but didn't want to give away too much information about herself. It was safer at the moment to let people only be aware of only one dimension of her aptitude.

"We should talk more later," said Kalina. "We still need to talk to Mark and Aisling about coming up with a recipe for the portal."

Robert led Kalina back to her own locker which she climbed through to get to her own headspace. Although the lockers here were wider than those in real life, she wondered what would happen if someone were too fat to get through. She didn't toy with the idea long before searching for Laurelle's book and hoping that she could find her door also.

Kalina remembered coming across Laurelle's book when she was looking for Mr. Wells. Had Robert not been there, she would have taken it off the shelf and placed it on the desk. All the same, she recalled the general location of the literature, and removed it from the shelf to examine. Like her door, the cover was plain and her name was unciphered, which was neither common nor uncommon among the psychic titles Kalina could peruse. Despite its plain exterior, it was no ordinary book. The pages inside were whiter than white such that it seemed that there had been no writing to begin with. *So there IS more to Laurelle than what meets the eye*, thought Kalina, who continued to examine the book in depth, searching for any hint, smudge, or mark that would have any meaning.

Disappointed that she couldn't see whatever message lay beyond the blank pages, Kalina eventually shut the book and decided to hunt for Laurelle's door, planning on entering her headspace like she did earlier that year. It didn't take long for her to find it given Laurelle's mental proximity (she was only a few doors away after all). However, Kalina hadn't noticed on her previous ventures into the hallway that Laurelle's door had changed. Had they not happened to cover fractals briefly in their geometry class, Kalina doubted that she would have recognized the upside-down Koch snowflake stamped upon Laurelle's door. Instead of having a hexagonal base, this crystal seemed to have five points that continuously pushed outwards. After taking a moment to trace the boundless perimeter, Kalina reached for the knob to open the door. To her chagrin, it wouldn't budge, and the more effort she put into opening it, the warmer the knob became until it was so hot she nearly burned herself. The eeriest part was the emergence of fragrant fumes coming from under the doorframe. It was too bad Kalina didn't pay more attention in biology; otherwise, she felt that she could have named the family of herbs being used. Instead, she panicked and took the only course of action she could think of: leaving the collective subconsciousness.

"What happened?" asked Maura, as Kalina snapped awake, her breath heavy and the fear of God in her eyes. "You look like you've seen a ghost!"

"Ugh," Kalina groaned as she sat up. If she had not felt so groggy, she would have rushed across the dorm to Laurelle's room to see if she could pick up a scent from her room. Instead, she slowly stood up and made her way across while addressing Maura. "There's something totally wrong with Laurelle. Let me check something; I'll be right back."

Kalina exited her room, leaving the dorm open. A few rooms down was Olympia's and Laurelle's room, which she knocked on. As if on cue, Laurelle greeted her from behind.

"Can I help you?" she asked, startling Kalina.

The chocolate-haired girl gave Kalina a half-smirk that made her skin crawl as she turned the key to enter her dorm.

"I was looking for you and Olympia. Maura and I were talking about trying to set up a date after break to study for finals. I thought we had some good momentum last time."

"Oh, I enjoyed it," replied Laurelle, whose tone was smug and whose lips dripped with a sincereness so intense that it almost sounded facetious.

If Laurelle was trying to put up an innocent facade, it was no longer working for Kalina. *That's fine,* she thought to herself. *Two can play that game.*

"Great," confirmed Kalina, in the sweetest voice she could muster. "I'll text the groupchat."

"Sounds like a plan. Well, I've got to start packing to go home for Thanksgiving break. I'll see you when we get back."

Laurelle closed the door behind her and Kalina strode back to the sanctuary of her own dormitory, unnerved by the encounter. Her feet uneasy, Kalina crashed into her chair like a boulder on the precipice of a cliff.

"Well?" prompted Maura, who was clearly anxious to be debriefed on the whole operation.

"I think Laurelle knows I was in there trying to enter her subconscience," began Kalina, who explained the situation with their former roommate first. She then went on to discuss the abnormalities of Mr. Wells' psychic presence. Kalina continued, "There's more. I've been having visions of him. It's like he's melting into the ground, but I don't know what that's about. In the past, my visions were a little more clearcut if a little bit hazy. The ones I've been having recently are chaotic. I saw him as a baby, and I think there's some sort of switched at birth thing going on."

Maura gasped at the last part, causing Kalina to raise her eyebrows. As though she were embarrassed, Maura closed her mouth immediately and her expression deepened into a state of consideration. Kalina patiently waited for her to write, erase, and rewrite whatever narrative she was coming up with. There was a lot of material to deal with, and Kalina herself struggled to connect the dots. Perhaps she would have had an easier time weaving what she learned together with her prescient aptitude once she rested and her magical energy were restored. Finally, Maura spoke up.

"What I'm about to say will sound ridiculous, but do you think that Mr. Wells could be a changeling?"

"I don't know what that is," admitted Kalina.

"It's like when the fair folk replace a human baby with one of their own. They then take the baby back into their world and keep it," she explained.

"Are faeries even real?" countered Kalina.

"Yes! Aisling has met them, and no she's not crazy. Faeries are descended from angels that have fallen for not taking a side in the spiritual war. At least, that's one theory of their origin."

"Let's not get too esoteric," pleaded Kalina, who considered Christianity to be one of her main identities. Talk of spirits and spiritual matters were best brought to a priest, her parents, or some other spiritual authority in her opinion. "Robert says that he'll ask Dr. Toumi about it. I'm more concerned with whatever is going on with Laurelle. Speaking of Robert, we're going to meet Saturday morning for breakfast to discuss plans for entering the library. *THE* library - not the one in my head I mean."

***

The mess hall was never particularly crowded before Thanksgiving break, and it was known that several students would spend Friday night in Winterburg with their parents before heading home. As a matter of fact, that's what Olympia said she was doing, which may explain Laurelle's toying behavior last night - she had caught Kalina in a fib.

Breakfast had consisted largely of leftovers from last night's Thanksgiving buffet, which pleased Kalina since she wasn't able to try all the desserts, many of which were strangers to her own family's traditional table. Discarding all notions of temperance that she should have kept during the Nativity fast, Kalina piled her tray with an assortment of pies, pastries, and pumpkin trifle. For a few minutes, it was just her and Maura, and although Kalina knew that

Aisling and Mark would be late, she was still irritated at their tardiness. Robert was the next to arrive, but didn't have any news about Mr. Wells. Although Maura suggested bringing it up with Aisling, Robert recommended that it would be better to solve one mystery at a time. Mr. Wells didn't seem to be an immediate concern, and he wanted to go to his mentor about the issue first before bringing other people in and potentially starting rumors. Eventually, Aisling and Mark came in hand and hand, greeting their friends before getting their breakfast trays.

"So," began Aisling. "What kind of progress have we made since our last meeting about a month ago?"

"We're trying to adjust the recipe," said Kalina. "Honestly, a lot of it is above my head since they don't even teach us how to cast our own spells yet. I was trying to reach out to you guys in the hope of you coming together to work something out. I did make a rudimentary IPO chart based on the techniques I read in my mom's paper."

"That's really good," praised Mark. "I've been looking into what you said about these little cuts and how a navigator can project a direction onto them instead *feeling* the direction from them, which is how my aptitude normally works."

Kalina was glad that Mark was softening up to the idea, especially since he was one of the harsher critics of her. In the end, it made her more resilient and clearly directed her to what she needed to work on.

"As for me," stated Kalina. "I'll need a spell so that I can perceive where these tiny cuts are going to appear, then Robert will use his telekinesis to expand the portal. Maura herself will have to use her acoustic aptitude in order to stabilize the portal at a certain resonance."

Mark tightened his face before turning to Aisling, saying "Well, you're the better spell-maker. Do you think this is possible?"

"Give me the chart and some preliminary examples of recipes and I should be able to come up with something that might work," she claimed. "The only other thing we'll need to do is decide a time to meet in order to perform the incantation. I suggest the solstice. We'll all be on break, plus our magic might be aided by the astrological weather."

"Where will we meet, though?" asked Kalina. "We all live so far apart, and Robert lives all the way in New Jersey!"

"Mark, do you think you parents would be willing to drive up to the Christmas market?" asked Aisling.

"Yeah, it's not too far away from Charlottesville, but then we still have to make sure Robert gets there. I hate to admit this, but he's vital to the incantation."

"He'll figure it out," said Aisling, finalizing their plan.

They continued the conversation lightly, occasionally bouncing around ideas and theories that they would look into, but at 10:07, Kalina received a text from her parents that they were ten minutes away. Knowing that she would spend her morning in the mess hall with her friends, she had already packed for Thanksgiving break. Thus, as soon her parents arrived, they were ready to depart. It was not the silent drive to school at the beginning of the semester, and although they were not listening to the radio, Kalina was happy to listen to the sound of Byzantine chanting.

"How have the past few weeks been? I know you're happy with Mr. Wells, but I want to know how your other classes are going," prompted Catherine.

"They're going pretty well. I like math and language arts. I thought I would like biology, but my teacher is kind of mean."

"Mrs. Blackwell," stated Catherine in an understanding tone. Kalina hadn't thought about this before, but Dean Schulz had her as his teacher, and that meant her mother did, too. Of course, she didn't bring up her new knowledge of their juvenile relationship, but the reminder did make her gulp.

"Yes," continued Kalina. "But I've been studying with my friends. That reminds me, we want to meet together at the D.C. Christmas Market over winter break."

"That sounds like a splendid idea," agreed her mom, but she heard her dad sigh, knowing that he would be the one to have to drive through the traffic and find parking.

"Let us know when, so we can do it," he said graciously, and Kalina was grateful to have such a patient father.

"We seem to all be free on the twenty-second. Does that work?"

Ivan took his eyes off the road to briefly look at his wife for confirmation, and she declared, "Yes, but we're going to be in the middle of the fast. By the way, we're not going to do a big turkey and everything for Thanksgiving this year because we'll be keeping to the Advent fast. This is a decision your father and I came to together."

Kalina was content either way. She had already got to have her big Thanksgiving feast at school. Plus, she was happy that her parents were able to find peace in their faith. It certainly has enabled them to be more tolerable since the summer.

***

The drive was long and tiring for Mark, who desperately wished that he had his best friend there to teleport him. Instead, he killed time by reading his textbook and listening with his mom to whatever news was on the radio. At least he had the turkey hunt to look forward to, and he would get his wrestling gear packed up for the next season. However, when he got home, he did not just greet his dad, but was surprised at the presence of Detective Christie.

"Oh, hello, sir," greeted Mark, who desperately wanted to interrogate him about why he decided to show up. A small anxiety crept in him about the detective's purpose here, but he quickly shoved that away. This man's eyes held a scrupulousness in them that forced Mark to remain as calm as a cucumber despite all odds.

"Hello, Mark. How has school been treating you? No further incidents I hope," responded Detective Christie.

Mark wanted to glare at him in response. He hated when adults left those snide remarks that were only seemingly innocent. Nevertheless, Mark knew that he had to play the game if he was going to have a chance at keeping his quasi-legal activities to himself. He might even gain more information.

"No, nothing at all. Is that why you're here? Has something happened?"

"Detective Christie had hired me onto his investigative team," answered his father. "This is just a casual dinner we're going to have."

"I thought you worked in linguistics processing for signals intelligence," pushed Mark, hoping to milk some more words about exactly what they were doing.

"Well, because of your my proximity to you, we've been looking into the cabal that Cara - Ms. Dalton was a part of -"

"But that's work stuff," interrupted Detective Christie. "I don't want you to worry about all that unless you have anything that you remember or learned at school that you think could help us in this case."

"I will, sir," promised Mark, who was put to ease now that he knew the reason behind Detective Christie's visit. He excused himself to put his bags away, but hid there until dinner time.

While his mother was away, his father took the liberty of buying groceries from the store for grilling. His brothers, Andrew and Matthew, arrived with some beer, which Mark wasn't allowed to have (in front of his parents), but he enjoyed the festive atmosphere. He knew that his father had cast an enchantment on either the burgers or the grill because they were much moister than usual. Naturally, he was trying to impress his new boss, but Mark was more focused on actually being able to enjoy a homemade burger. That was until Detective Christie started asking him questions.

"So, Mark," he began unobtrusively. "You're a junior, right? What are your plans for after you graduate?"

"I'm applying to the Naval Academy in Annapolis," answered Mark, wondering where this conversation was headed.

"Oh, I know some people over there. It's a tough school to get into, but maybe I could put in a good word for you, especially since you were so helpful in the investigation earlier this year."

Although he spoke of a promise, Mark sensed an underlying threat beneath his words. Of course what he meant by this year was last school year, when the whole fiasco of Ms. Dalton went down. Mark hesitated to utter a thanks due to the perceived insincerity in the detective's dark words, but before anything could be said, he continued.

"I was very impressed when the dean told me that you students were not only researching the enchanted forest, but had actually ventured out into it *and* returned safe and sound."

"Ye-e-s," stuttered Mark, calculating his next sentence. "It was an incredible achievement outside the circumstances."

"Really," mused the detective. "I think you were exceptionally brave given the circumstances. That is, the kidnapping of Kalina Todorova. It's remarkable that you found her. A simple footprint tracking spell! I wish I had thought of that... Well, actually I did. While you three were rescuing Kalina, forensics was scanning the area around the woods, and guess what? There were no footprints save yours. Carannog would not have been so careless as to leave evidence of the kidnapping. Besides, you yourself said in your school report that the spatial dimensions of the Enchanted Forest shift unpredictably. So, either you have one hell of a footprint spell, or you've been lying to us. I highly doubt the first one is true, and the second one... Well, let's just say that getting into Annapolis will be the least of your worries."

Mark's heart began to beat faster and faster, but he noted an interesting lapse in Christie's narrative. Unable to think of anything else to say at the moment, he blurted, "Who's Carannog?"

"One of Dalton's names, but you still have to answer the question."

The whole table silently stared at Mark waiting for him to respond, and in that moment the whole world seemed to collapse around him. Was there a ringing in his ears? He could have sworn there was cotton in his throat.

"Well, if you don't tell me," pushed Detective Christie. "I might have to bring you in for obstruction of justice. However, if you do tell me the truth, perhaps I can do you a favor in return. Maybe it'd be better if we did this in private."

Mark nodded his head as if he had a choice, and since it was his father's house, he led them upstairs into his office to continue the conversation. Mark requested his father stay, desperate for support and any sort of protection he could provide in the aftermath of the confession. Still, Mark struggled to get the words out, causing frustration in Detective Christie.

"Oh for goodness sake, give him something to drink, Norman. I'm not the normie police, I don't care about that stuff."

His father wasn't as prudish about his mom about drinking, though he respected her rules for the way she ran her household. That being said, this was a unique situation that supported a bending of the norm. Norman pulled out a glass bottle of enchanted firejack from under the desk and poured some for his son.

"It's going to burn," he warned.

"Have you ever had anything to drink?" asked the detective, but Mark shook his head and took a whiff of the strong beverage. "No, not even at school? You kids are boring these days. My advice, take it all at once. It's just like ripping off a bandage."

Despite the discomfort Detective Christie had flung upon Mark, he had no reason to distrust the man, and took a big swig of the cinnamon-flavored liquid. It burned at first, not like the way he expected. It was *spicy*, not just on his tongue but he felt it all throughout his veins. Unlike chili powder, the pain went away after a few moments, leaving Mark all warm and fuzzy on the inside. He understood why magi made this drink; it calmed the nerves even if it did make him a little groggy. By the time he put his glass down, his father had prepared ones for himself and Detective Christie.

"Now, son, why don't you tell Detective Christie over here what really happened that day. I can't promise you won't be in trouble, but we need to know."

Mark took a deep breath and began from the moment they learned of Kalina's disappearance. There was a heroic element to be sure - they did rescue the girl after all, but they still used illegal blood magic to do it. A part of him was ashamed of the fact that he threw Aisling under the bus since it was she who suggested and retrieved the recipe, but who could blame Phillip? It was his *sister* who was in grave danger. It took some effort not to be loquacious, but he resisted going further than discovering Kalina. However, something told Mark that if Detective Christie knew about Dalton's history - what did he call her? Caronga? - then he likely knew a lot more than he was letting on.

"And Kalina, the poor girl, how has she taken it so far?" asked his father, likely trying to cast a positive light upon Mark, who would fumble the opportunity.

"She's obsessed with finding Phillip," answered Mark, who was feeling the influence of the firejack more intensely now. He wished he had never taken a sip of it. "We made plans to go into the library to find him. She thinks we can do it. Don't worry, dad; I already talked to mom."

"Tell me about his library," prompted the detective, who remained as cool as a computer.

"I doubt that it will actually work," began Mark, who started spitting off facts about their extracurricular research. Whether or not the two men were actually interested, Mark couldn't tell. In fact he couldn't tell what he was saying at all - or what they were saying to each other except for bits of pieces. The last thing he heard was, "his brothers weren't like this their first time having a drink."

***

Despite her claim to not celebrate Thanksgiving, Catherine Todorova couldn't help but prepare a fasting friendly feast, and Kalina was more than happy to help her mother. Thus, they prepared Swedish-styled salmon, garlic mashed potatoes, green beans, stuffing, roasted sweet potatoes, and honey glazed carrots for dinner. Kalina herself was surprised as to how many of their classic dishes they could prepare with a few simple adjustments, and their kitchen was large enough to make all the dishes. For dessert, they made a simple pumpkin pie with a pecan crust. No self-respecting Virginian would have a sweet potato pie instead.

Full and sleepy from dinner, Kalina headed upstairs to her room for some peace and quiet. The combined effort of cooking, eating, and cleaning had worn her out, and she was ready to lay down in her soft, twin-sized bed. She missed the sensation of the memory foam, which allowed her to sink into a deeper sleep, and she wondered if she could use this to her advantage with her aptitude. After scrolling on her phone a bit, she put on some binaural beats, hoping to be carried into the plane of the collective subconsciousness without Maura's help.

Unfortunately, it hadn't worked, and when Kalina opened her eyes, she saw only the dim state of her room. Since she didn't have anything better to do, she reached for her phone but her finger tips passed through it. Startled, she turned around to see her body lying still on her mattress. It wasn't just that her room was dark, but there was a bluish tint to it, informing her that she was having an out of body experience. Although she had entered into this state of being before, it wasn't something that had come up often, and she never asked either Dr. Toumi or Robert about what it meant. Out of the corner of her eye, she thought she saw movement, and quickly twisted to catch what it was. It seemed to only be the silhouette of her laundry piled onto her chair.

It's okay, she told herself in order to calm down. Still, she recalled Sister Maryam's warning about entering these spaces as well as Robert's warning about mysterious entities that exist in the aerial plane. *I still have to be brave.* Instead of going back to her body, she headed downstairs to observe her parents, who weren't doing anything interesting except watching the news. More specifically, her mom watched the news while her dad lay asleep on the couch.

In her boldness, Kalina exited the house, and though the streets were dark, she could still perceive the blue tinge through the various street lights. Remembering Robert's hypothesis that her aptitude had mixed with her brother's, she wondered if she could teleport to different places in the aerial realm. *Who would I go see first? Not Maura, since I've already invaded her privacy once. Definitely Laurelle, though.* As Kalina walked through the cul-de-sac, she pondered on Laurelle and her motives. What was she up to? Why wasn't she being honest with Kalina? Where was she right now?

Suddenly, Kalina noticed that she was in an unfamiliar part of her neighborhood, which surprised her because she often took walks with her parents after dinner or throughout the day. The house before her, however, was irrecognizable. In fact, there were no townhouses in her neighborhood, which meant that she would have had to cross one of the main roads to get to them. As her heart stammered for a second, believing she was lost, the crimson door of the middle townhouse opened, revealing a familiar face that was taking out the trash.

Laurelle! gasped Kalina, but her voice didn't resonate in the air. *I did it! I teleported here without having to map out the navigation!*

Thinking neither of the implications nor of the consequences of her actions, Kalina raced up the stairs to the townhouse, hoping to get a peak of her former roommate's home life. Before she entered, she wanted to check if there were any wards that would have harmed her or alarmed the residents. She tried casting an incantation, but because her voice didn't work in the aerial realm, she tried the hand gesture that her father showed her. She tried, and tried again, but couldn't figure out how to work it in the aerial realm. Instead, Kalina tried to figure out the other techniques that her mother mentioned, but she couldn't remember anything. Ultimately, with a leap of faith, she stepped through the bounds of the house, entering the minimalist space of Kalina's family.

Kalina couldn't smell anything, but upon entering the kitchen, she observed that they were cleaning up after an intimate Thanksgiving dinner. It seemed to have just been the three of them - the immediate family, which made Kalina curious as to their relations with their extended members. Like her own home, this house was silent except for the tv, and like Kalina, Laurelle headed up to her own room after finishing her chores. As Kalina followed her up the short staircase, she witnessed the walls swirling in her shadows. Still, she hoped this was an anomaly, and continued to follow Laurelle to her room. By now, the wispy shapes had grown thicker on the walls, making Kalina nervous to enter Laurelle's room. However, when she reached the boundary, she was blocked by a ward that appeared to her in a star-shaped design similar to Laurelle's door in the collective subconsciousness. As she backed up, Laurelle quickly turned to look at her with a grimace that mixed perplexity and worry. The only relieving quality of the situation was that Laurelle did not seem to perceive Kalina, who was now beginning to be enveloped in total darkness. Panicking, Kalina very nearly cried out to her mother and could only wish for the safety of her home. When it seemed nearly too late, Kalina snapped up from her bed and immediately reached to her nightstand to find her Rubik's cube, which she hadn't used in several weeks. She solved every one she had, but was still scared of falling back asleep. She was sure that she had witnessed nefarious aerial entities that were clustered in Laurelle's home, so with faith and trembling she ran to her small icon corner and prayed fervently for God's protection.

29
FINALS AND TRIALS

Academic achievement was always a matter of diligence and not difficulty for Kalina. Unfortunately for her, distractions had entered her mind from every corner during the semester - from Robert to Phillip to Dalton, and so on, she felt like she could not catch a break. No wonder the temptation to put herself to rest with binaural beats was so strong. It felt like the only path to putting her mind to rest and finding answers.

It's not a disregard of Sister Maryam's warning, she said to herself. *I'm aware of the dangers now, but I still need to face it. If I could survive those malicious entities once, I can do it again if I need to, and I'll be prepared next time.* Even as she tried to assure herself, she wasn't entirely sure that she believed in it. In any case, she maintained that she would stick with what she knew to be safe and practiced.

Before she could meditate on the very real scare, she reigned in her meandering mind back to her studies. Taking a peak to her left, Maura was working on the same set of practice problems that Miss Haverty had printed out for them. Her best friend had promised her that her sister had been working diligently on developing the recipes, but Aisling hadn't reached out yet.

"Isn't it nice that they gave us a period of studying after break before they throw a week of intense examination at us?" asked Kalina, who really didn't want to bother studying at the moment. It was as though she couldn't reign in the constant hooting and hollering of her brain, wishing to swing from topic to topic and never reaching the subject before her.

"It wouldn't be so bad if we didn't have to also turn in homework and projects," replied Maura, who kept scribbling down answers.

"I'm bored," confessed Kalina. "I can't concentrate on homework after break. Nothing feels real, and I can't stop thinking about what we're going to do on the solstice."

"Like I said, Aisling's working on it," said Maura simply before returning to her work.

Kalina, overcome by the evening's spirit of ennui, considered telling Maura about her experience with Laurelle. Although she had plenty of to think about the incident, she hadn't yet come to a decision. Tonight, however, she would let her impulse get to her, and boldly spoke up again.

"I never told you about my experience with Laurelle over break. I have some major tea to spill," began Kalina, who watched her roommate spin around once more to engage in conversation. The homework could wait; the report was more important. "I needed some time to process what happened, but I think you could help me figure it out."

Maura leaned forward, emerald eyes wide open, and her jaw rested in between her palms.

"Well, go on," she urged.

Kalina recounted her foray into the astral realm, and the two discussed the implications of the shadowy figures Kalina encountered. Moreover, they briefly discussed the harmonic techniques used to induce psychic experiences, but they were especially worried about Laurelle's agenda.

"Have you told Robert about it yet? He would know more than I do."

"Not yet. I was waiting for Aisling so that I could tell everyone at once," answered Kalina, hoping to expedite the waiting period.

"Let me text her right now," appeased Maura, reaching for her phone. She was a quick typer, and luckily for them, Aisling was a quick responder. "She said we could meet tomorrow to begin the testing phase.

***

The next day, Kalina got up later than usual. She had recently found herself becoming more and more of a night person, which was atypical of herself. Maura, on the other hand, was up bright and early. Although she was seated at her desk in an attempt to continue their homework, she seemed to have devolved into doomscrolling on Magigram.

Kalina groggily shifted her legs out of bed, and without saying anything to Maura, immediately brushed her teeth. Sometimes, she simply was not in the mood to make conversation first thing in the morning. When she emerged, she found Maura in the same spot, not even glancing up at her roommate.

"What time does your sister want to meet?"

"She said we'll meet after lunch, so around 12:30," responded Maura, who continued to scroll.

Kalina was fine with that, and at least she now had a time table to look forward to while she accomplished some minor tasks. This time, she did end up using the spell book they gave the seventh graders, and she finished her chores in no time.

"Don't use too much of your magic," warned Maura. "You'll need it for testing."

"I know," sighed Kalina. She had already ironed and folded her laundry, made her bed, shined her shoes, and freshened up her room. That was enough for today, and it was already approaching noon. Kalina announced, "Lunch should start being served by the time we walk over. Let's go."

Maura obliged, and the two walked over to the mess hall. It was the perfect day to do some casting. The sky was clear, the air was crisp, and autumn weather was in full effect. Instead of eating inside, Maura and Kalina took their sandwiches outside and sat on the lawn where they would be meeting the others. As it happened, Mark and Aisling had the same idea, and caught up with the two girls to chow down together. The only person missing was Robert, and Kalina anxiously checked her phone to see if he sent any updates.

"I'm sure he'll turn up after he's finished lunch. He's probably in the mess hall," assured Aisling, who began taking out materials.

Kalina was sure that they looked like an odd medley to the average passerby - a wrestler, a cheerleader, two middle-schoolers, and now approaching, the former quarterback and football player.

"Right on time," stated Aisling. "I was just about to hand out the recipes. I printed them out fresh this morning in the library."

"Which part of the spell is up to me?" asked Maura impatiently.

"I highlighted it for each person. I think you have to flip the page to see yours. The front is the order in which we have to do it," explained Aisling. "I also brought snacks. We'll need them. Kalina, you're first, and the whole spell relies on you. So, no pressure or anything."

Kalina nodded her head, examining her paper, the top of which was highlighted. Aisling's idea was not to open a portal to the library, but to perceive and stabilize a random "Wheeler" wormhole, which made her clairvoyant aptitude necessary. The problem was that Kalina wasn't used to using her abilities at such a microscopic level - quite the opposite actually. Seeing Kalina's tensed face, Aisling spoke up.

"I'm sorry, I couldn't find a lot of material on making recipes for your aptitude, especially not for such a modern and niche subject. I did put some ideas down, though."

Kalina had already examined the points, heavy with scientific language. If there were a geometry or a foamlike pattern, that may help her visualize their appearance.

"Sorry, I just need a second," she said, interrupting her own thoughts.

"Take your time," answered Mark respectfully. "We also need to examine our parts, and it looks like you have one of the harder ones."

Kalina thought about the miniscule bridges, and their disturbances in reality. From time to time, she felt like she could see the fabric of reality itself, but she was never able to harness it. There would need to be environmental circumstances that heightened her aptitude - the yarn, the football game, the test - and even then she didn't have full control over it. *Disturbances, little disturbances*, she meditated.

She took out a quarter that Mr. Wells had given her and popped it into the air. She saw it as it left her fingers - tails. However, she perceived, as if in slow motion, the random probability distortions that occurred around the coin. When the coin landed on her palm, it was still tails, but her aptitude had caught up with her in the form of a migraine, causing her to sit down.

"Kalina!" exclaimed Aisling, bringing her a bottle of water and a bag of chips. "Are you alright? Do I need to call for a medical emergency?"

"I'm fine," responded Kalina. "I think I tried something new with my aptitude. Do you think that wormholes can cause probability distortions?"

"That would make sense," answered Aisling. "Given that they have rippling effects on reality they intrude upon. Do you think you can perceive the wormholes through these effects?"

"Maybe, but it's going to take a lot. I'm sorry. I used up some of my magic earlier while doing chores."

"That's fine," said Aisling gently. "I wasn't expecting us to open up any wormholes today to be honest. Plus, we can all practice our incantations without one. You just rest up."

Kalina sat on the cold grass as she drank her water, observing what everyone else was doing. Aisling and Mark were hovered over the paper with a compass, likely making trigonometric calculations. Maura seemed to be enjoying herself, humming seemingly innocently into the air, but if Kalina looked hard enough, she could observe the harmonic patterns she was creating with the various atmospheric molecules. Robert himself seemed to be toying with the air, but she couldn't see what it was that he was doing. Not only was he in charge of telepathically connecting her sight to everyone else in the spell, he was in charge of telekinetically expanding the wormhole once they had stabilized it through Mark and Maura.

Robert noticed her watching him, and he headed over. Maura herself took note of the occurrence but continued having fun with her incantations.

"You look like you have something on your mind," he pointed out.

"You're right," confirmed Kalina, who then gave him a brief retelling of the events with Laurelle. "I know you told me about there being non-human entities in these realms, but why were they all surrounding Laurelle. Are they like demons or something?"

"I don't know, but what you're telling me is serious. I know you're afraid of engaging with these beings or going to a 'mentor' for help because of last year, so if you don't mind, give me some time to figure it out."

"I don't want to get in trouble either," pleaded Kalina.

"Don't worry. To be honest, this may be an after winter break investigation. Let's just focus on finding your brother first."

Kalina agreed with him, and when she later told Maura, she also concurred. The rest of the day went well, and the starchy bag of potato chips gave Kalina more energy to work with. As Kalina worked with Robert to telepathically share the distortions she was seeing in reality, Aisling rapidly took notes.

"I think I have enough data to work with," stated Aisling enthusiastically. "Keep practicing Kalina, and we'll definitely get a clean look at a wormhole."

No one was upset at departing from the grounds, as they were all fatigued from using significant amounts of magic that day. Kalina, who had picked up a bit of a sweat, was looking forward to taking a hot shower and laying down. After they checked back in, she and Maura followed their typical routine, and while Maura went in to rinse off after her, Kalina adjusted her pillow to lie down in, and immediately fell asleep.

30

A HOLE IN THE SOLSTICE

The Magical Christmas Market in D.C. isn't actually held in D.C. In the seventies, the USDM had decided that it was far too risky to have the Magical Christmas Market right next to the regular one after an elderly woman had somehow found herself in the midst of several magi unaware of her presence. Fortunately for both the community and the woman, she had already been diagnosed with Alzheimer's, which made any sort of memory inhibiting magic unnecessary.

Kalina's parents didn't often go to the Christmas Market, instead choosing to stay at home with family, but Kalina's ulterior motives led her to ask for an exception. Of course her parents acquiesced since it wasn't really too far from where they lived anyways.

As soon as they parked, Kalina texted the group chat with Aisling, Mark, Maura, and Robert that she had arrived. It seemed as though everyone was there, except for Aisling and Maura, who were about fifteen minutes away. Kalina wished that she would be able to enjoy some of the activities, but knew that she would be too anxious until they completed their mission. Upon entering, she immediately caught Robert and Mark munching on some pastries. She pointed them out to her parents before jogging up to greet them.

"How can you guys eat right now?" asked Kalina. "Aren't you nervous?"

"A little," replied Robert. "That's *why* I'm eating. And you should, too. You're going to want enough calories to cast the spell."

"Same here," added Mark. "Aisling said that she's going to be a little longer anyways, so we might as well have a look around before we have our adventure."

Kalina was surprised that Robert and Mark were getting along so well and even their parents. She wondered if Mark's parents were aware that he had resented Robert for dating Aisling for so long. Robert bought Kalina a bratwurst, which she nibbled on while she waited. None of them were particularly chatty, though all six of their parents seemed to be getting along well. Instead, Kalina decided to watch the crowd, noticing the abundance of security added since last year's attack. They still hadn't discovered the perpetrators or the motive. Or if they had, the information wasn't public yet.

Soon enough, Mark stood on his tippy-toes and started waving to someone. In the distance, Kalina caught the group of gingers entering the market. Immediately, Maura sprinted over to embrace Kalina, and Aisling jogged along behind her.

She briefly looked at her peers up and down, and said, "Well, there's no point in waiting around. Let's get this show on the road."

Kalina obliged, and the group moved along, twisting itself around the organic crowd. When she briefly looked behind her, she saw the parents talking to each other, but something was off. Although the atmosphere of the market was jovial, there seemed to be a sober umbra clouding everyone. Maybe it was just the heavy security she was noticing and the memory of last year's attack.

Anyways, they eventually found a somewhat secluded alley where they could perform the complicated spell. Silver shivers ran down Kalina's spine as she embraced the meteorological impact of the cold moon, a feeling similar to when she prophesied over a year ago at the football game. For a moment, the dots started to connect, and she felt the history of the place she was in, just as she had done with Mr. Wells - the past, the present, the future. Before she was too far lost, she felt someone poking at her brain. She let Robert in, and felt him connect her to the rest of the group. This was the first time they had practiced the telepathic connection, and she saw that no one except Maura was confident that the incantation would *really* work. Yet, these points started to connect, and just as Dalton produced a web connecting their class, so too could Kalina see the fabric of space weaving around them. Little bubbles seemed to carbonate the atmosphere surrounding them, and Kalina, taking a deep breath, was able to see into the foam. Instead of trying to chase one of these capricious pockets down, she focused her attention on one spot in front of her, waiting for the subatomic hole to occur. Eventually, it did, and it felt like she had to hold onto it for several seconds before Maura and Mark would be able to stabilize it. With a gasp, she was finally able to let go, and the world returned to its normal pace. Except, Maura's harmonic rhythm flooded the atmosphere with a heightened sense of stability and ambient presence. Kalina, still a part of the telepathic connection, could sense when Mark had projected the direction of the wormhole orthogonally to their present reality, and immediately she was cut off. Robert would have to act rapidly and would need all the magic he could possibly muster in order to expand the hole for them to travel through it.

At first slowly, then exponentially, the hole started to grow. Aisling, impulsive and brave as ever, was the first to go through. Maura was next, then Kalina, then Mark, who was a little more hesitant. Finally, Robert entered, and the hole collapsed behind him. Before it closed, Kalina spotted men rushing towards them, and heard echoes of shouts. Next to her, Robert had crumpled to the ground, looking pale.

"Are you alright," asked Kalina, worried that he had overextended himself. He nodded that he was fine and stated that he just needed a second to get his bearings. Meanwhile, the rest of the crew was admiring their surroundings.

"Wow," gasped Aisling. "It's beautiful!"

"It doesn't look like the same place," noted Kalina. "I guess there are different sections, but the last time I was here the structure was marble not wood."

Despite the difference in space, which was more claustrophobic and maze-like, though still just as messy, Kalina was sure that they were in the right place.

"That's weird," stated Mark. "It feels like for the first time, I don't know where I am."

"That's your aptitude acting up, trying to make sense of where we are," answered Kalina. "I think this place is a kind of paradox.

There's space here, but it's still a pocket of voidness. Come on, let's figure out how to get out of this section."

They all moved together, afraid of getting lost. Eventually, Aisling pointed out a doorway that led them to a space that looked much more familiar. White marbled floors with neatly lined shelves, and in the distance, a desk.

"That looks like the front, if there is such a thing," said Robert, who opted to stay in the back.

The desk had several stacks of books on it, and a bell, which Kalina assumed summoned assistance, but hesitated to press it.

"Shall we ring it?" asked Aisling, but Kalina shook her head. Something had felt off about it to her.

"I wouldn't if I were you," said a voice behind them, causing them all to jump. "Sorry to frighten you," continued the elderly man, who had placed another pile of books on the desk. "You all seem new here. Who's the traveler?"

"None of us are travelers," answered Robert, whose complexion remained unnervingly white. "We were able to get here without one."

"That should not be possible," responded the graying man, with eyes squinting sharply at them, trying to perceive any malice.

"It is," affirmed Kalina. "My brother is a traveler, and he sent me here once by accident, and I had to get back without him. He's missing, and I thought I might be able to find him here."

The older man sighed with sympathy, "I can't promise that you'll be able to find him in this place, and I worry that you will all get lost. However, I will do my best to help you. In fact, I know several of the travelers here who I can ask. Why, I'm helping one right now. He's around here somewhere. Oh, look!"

"Phillip!" shouted Kalina, as soon as she saw his figure emerge from a row of bookshelves. There was a shorter, blonde girl walking next to him, dressed in a white stola. Behind them was a small group of a few other students dressed in crimson attire, but Kalina didn't recognize them.

"Kalina?"

As soon as they recognized the other, they rushed to hug each other, Kalina's trying not to let her tears cloud her eyes. Phillip himself seemed relieved, and she realized that he had no idea whether or not she was able to escape Dalton last year.

"You're taller than I remembered," said Phillip.

"You look older," replied his sister.

Kalina was ecstatic to see her brother once more and accomplish her mission. However, the experience was short-lived when the girl in the stola pointed out several dark figures emerging from another room.

"This should *not* be possible," restated the older man. "What kind of traveler could have invited *them* into the Museum?"

"You could thank the two siblings before you," answered the tall woman who walked

in the middle. "They need to learn to be more careful with their life force."

"You!" yelped the girl in the stola.

"*Me?* I'm afraid I've lived a long life, so don't be offended if I don't recognize you," snickered the tall, swarthy woman. This only made the girl turn beet red with ire.

"You tried to have me killed for being a Christian!"

"To be honest, that only narrows it down from the non-Christians I have killed, which is strange because I'm normally successful in my murder-rate. Hmmm... Oh wait, you're the Vestal Virgin who got away! For several centuries I wondered where you went. I guess I finally have my answer," Dido smirked. "And an opportunity to take care of an unfinished job!"

Dido raised her hand, signaling for her minions to attack the group, and although they were outnumbered, they had the fortunate advantage of being on uncertain territory. Here, magic didn't work properly, and the layout of space was convoluted. Nonetheless, several of the students scattered in fear. The Roman girl had taken Phillip by the hand and led him and his new friends away, leaving Kalina to figure out how to take care of herself. Luckily, the older Roman man was skilled enough to manipulate the bookshelves and hold off the attackers long enough for Kalina's aptitude to kick in, and she directed her companions to follow suit.

She was running completely on instincts, but had to trust herself to get everyone to safety. Meanwhile, the shady figures pursued the teens casting all sorts of hexes and curses at them. Robert shielded them by using his telekinesis to control obstacles and even sent some books flying in their opponents' direction. Some tried to burn them, but nothing would catch fire. After meandering for ages through the bookshelves while never straying too far from their point of origin,

Kalina started to become out of breath. Despite the adrenaline rush, she began to tire out and her aptitude seemed to become more uncertain when it came to her sense of self-preservation. Robert (who himself had started to become fatigued) was teamed with Aisling in holding off the ambush, while Maura looked to Kalina for instruction. For a moment, Kalina felt more fear than she ever had before - it was the gut-wrenching type that meant the butterflies in your stomach had grown claws and were ripping their way out. Then it was gone, and Kalina knew it was a premonition. With the aid of Aisling, Robert had finally subdued one of Dido's followers, and then the most piercing ring echoed through infinity - somebody had decided to ring the bell. Though she already felt it herself, she could see among her allies that same terror which foreshadowed destruction. The only convenience was that it caused the cloaked figure to collapse.

The environment had taken a turn for the worse when the light dimmed to a deep, sanguine red, and materiality began to melt around them, starting with the bookshelves. As the shelf to her left melted to the floor, Kalina took sight of the aetherial sliver that opened up to the D.C. Market, and she immediately connected the purpose of her instincts.

"There!" she shouted at her recovering friends, directing them back to the safety of a regular plane of existence.

Robert understood and helped Aisling to her feet. Maura led the way, but Kalina stood in the back, hoping to catch sight of her brother. As the rest of the space bled into nothingness, including the very ground, she could see not only Dido's posse scrambling to escape, but at an angle above her, Phillip led his own entourage away from imminent danger. The older Roman man was nowhere to be found. At this point, her friends had crossed the portal to safety, but she wanted to make sure that Phillip would do the same. Even if they weren't entirely reunited, she had to know that he would make it out of here alive.

After several moments that seemed to take forever when under the pressure of approaching dematerialization (that had already claimed the lives of several of Dido's people), Phillip finally cut out a door that meant he would escape. At this point, the expanse of darkness was only a yard away from Kalina, who decided it was time to jump through the portal and meet her friends.

31

EMBITTERED AND BATTLED

Kalina slammed into the same small alley they had just departed from, Robert and Aisling appearing next. Her hands and knees scraped against the asphalt, but her adrenaline prevented her brain from registering the pain.

"That was *too* close," said Robert, covered in sweat, but not gasping for air anymore. Although his face was red with exertion, Kalina was glad to see the color return to him.

"It wasn't close enough," replied Kalina. "We got to Phillip, but he didn't come back with us."

"You kids actually did it," proclaimed a voice from behind them. "I'll admit; I am *shocked*, and that *does not* happen often."

Kalina turned around, recognizing the man in the suit.

"Detective Christie?" she began. "How did you know that we found Phillip?"

"I didn't, not until you just told me at least. I did know you were attempting to teleport, which I suppose is pretty cool."

Robert put a hand on Kalina's shoulder, bringing to her attention the armed guards that flanked him. The entrance to the alley was cut off with police tape, and there lingered a hooded, female figure.

It's Dalton, said Robert inside her head. *I think she and Detective Christie have been working together.*

"What's going on?" voiced Aisling immediately, and Kalina was starting to envision how this would all play out.

"Blood magic, pyromancy, possession, spirit magic, not to mention the unknown legality of whatever it is you just did" answered Detective Christie, accusing no one in particular. "You four are in some serious trouble, and I'm going to have to make some arrests."

Four? There were five of us in total, thought Kalian as she tried to calm herself, doing the best she could to muster the voice.

"No," she shouted. It was a mere shout, and she immediately realized that Robert had placed a magical wall over her. She looked at him with wide eyes, wondering why he betrayed her.

"No?" scoffed Detective Christie. "I'm afraid you don't have a choice in the matter."

Assuming that Kalina expected Robert to act and knowing how powerful he was, Detective Christie cast a spell on him first. It was silent, but Robert crumpled to the ground after a wave of his hand. It was a shame that he had already exhausted most of his magic; he might have actually stood a chance.

"What did you do to him?" yelled Aisling.

"Don't worry; he's just asleep. He's faced worse before. Now, am I going to have to do the same to the rest of you?"

Detective Christie stepped forward, already loading an incantation with his hand gestures. If he hadn't allied himself with the woman who tried to kill her and steal her magic, Kalina would have gone quietly.

"Explain yourself!" demanded Kalina, pointing to where Ms. Dalton had been waiting, watching the scene play out. After being revealed, she pulled her hood down and walked over to Detective Christie.

"I don't need to explain anything to *you*," he replied, and Kalina *hated* the disdain and condescension that seethed out of the detective's pearly white teeth.

Now that Robert was unconscious, the same wall he had placed on her had disappeared, and with all loathing, Kalina mustered up her aptitude to again command, "***EXPLAIN -***"

"None of that!" interrupted Detective Christie, who was sewing the air with his hands.

First, her throat began to close, and then she felt her lips being sewn shut by an ethereal string. Unable to breath or move her lips, Kalina sank to her knees in a panic. To her left, she faintly heard Aisling muttering an incantation in a foreign language, Irish, most likely.

"That's the one you need to watch out for," noted Cara Dalton, her voice now cold and raspy. "She's the one who's made a deal with one of the Tuatha."

For a few moments, Detective Christie turned his attention to Aisling, who was frantically reaching into her pockets in search of what Kalina guessed to be a magical card. It was plenty of time for Kalina to shut her eyes, to draw in and recenter herself.

We're here for you if you need us...

Kalina didn't have long enough to discern where the voices came from, and simply responded, *If you are truly friends of mine, come to my aid.* By the time she reopened her eyes, Aisling was gone, and Kalina had been surrounded by the detective and his armed guards. Mark was on the other side of the ring being led away with Maura, so it was just herself and Robert lying limp next to her. *Inhale slowly*, she told herself, but when she exhaled through her nose, plumes of smoke exited. The magical strings that Detective Christie had sewn over her lips melted away, and gray smoke started to exit from her mouth as well. It swirled around the guards and Ms. Dalton, darkening the atmosphere.

Kalina, gaining her strength, stood up, glared at the unbroken detective, who even now was struggling to maintain composure, and began to incant.

"I see most clear your cold desire tonight,
And playing games with made up rules no right,
Two can sew each others mouth and close it,
Your mind, your heart to me is now unwrit."

Kalina looked around her, each one of the guards lay pale on the floor. She hadn't wanted them to die, but at the end of the day, they were responsible for putting themselves in that situation. Only Dalton was left standing, and Kalina turned to face her.

"My prodigy," she began.

Before she could continue, however, Kalina directed the smoke through her fingers. A tornado of smoke encompassed Dalton, and when it dissipated, only a skull was left. Now that neither Detective Christie nor Dalton was now suppressing him, Robert regained consciousness.

"What happened?" he asked, seeing the dead bodies that surrounded him.

"After you were knocked out, Detective Christie attacked me. Aisling tried to defend herself. There was a commotion, and then... she was gone. I don't know what happened to her or where she went."

"These bodies, are they...?"

"Yes," stated Kalina tersely. "I didn't want it to happen, but they gave me no choice."

Robert began to back away from Kalina, and for the first second time she was able to glean his mental state. Fear oozed out of him.

"What happened to you?" he asked.

"What happened to me?" yelled Kalina back to him. "You're the one who blocked my aptitude. *You* almost compromised us completely. And now look!"

"No," said Robert, shaking his head. "This isn't right."

Perceiving that he would either call for help or try another telepathic enchantment on her, Kalina prepared to leave. *I can't fight him, but I can try to run away.* The voices that she had heard answered her, *you need only tell us where, Mistress, and we shall carry you there*. Grateful for the help, Kalina responded to them, and her world once again was enveloped by the ashen fumes.

EPILOGUE

Anxiety pressed upon Betty as she waited for Lucia to help Phillip in creating an escape portal, and Sally's increasingly violent sobs only increased her disorientation. After following Lucia through a space where gravity and the laws of physics seemingly had no meaning, Betty had become nauseous. To a curved wall on her right (well, it wasn't a wall, the plane of existence here was saddle-shaped), she could see Dido's followers barely making their evasion into a distant portal. Dido herself sacrificed many of her people in order to secure her existence. Finally, Phillip was able to dig a portal out with his hands, and Lucia was the first to enter. Although the abyss approached, Betty made sure the younger students - Nancy, Sally, and Glenn - made it to safety before her. Then, she jumped through just before Phillip did, greeted by an intense, biting cold.

The ground beneath her crunched, and her eyes had to adjust to the dim landscape that had been overtaken by fluttering snowflakes. She had never been good at using her aptitude in wintry weather, but she tried to draw warmth into herself as best as she could. When she saw her schoolmates shiver, she immediately stopped, afraid that she was drawing upon their body heat.

"Well, the good news is that we're back at school," noted Glenn, and Betty's own eyes confirmed the truth, taking note of the dormitories.

"Who's that?" exclaimed Sally, and when Betty turned around, she witnessed a large man approaching them. She knew the school faculty, and he was definitely not part of it. Instinctively, she raised her arms to protect her younger peers, ready to fend off another one of Dido's soldiers. Thinking quickly, Nancy formed a spell with her hands, melting a runic circle around them, to which Betty was grateful. Defensive magic wasn't her specialty, but when the steam of the snow dissipated, she could recognize the geometric shapes that the thoughtograph had formed.

It was excellent timing too, since just then, the muscular man, dressed in a thick overcoat and baggy sweatpants, had just arrived. Apart from his ski-mask and intimidating posture, the aggressive way he held his wand only reassured the young students that they had reason to fear him. Betty couldn't hear the words he spoke, as they were muffled by his balaclava, but when he raised his wand, she instinctively raised her hands in defense, drawing up whatever magic she had left in her.

***

"They're just kids," scolded Dr. Toumi, but Mr. Campbell just shrugged.

Mr. Wells had to admit that he sided with Mr. Campbell. There was just too much dark magic happening at the school as of late.

They were fortunate to have caught these kids on a day when the USDM had taken a break from their investigation for the Christmas holiday. All the kids were clearly frightened and too stunned to speak, but his main concern right now was helping Dean Schulz and Mr. Campbell lift up the girl in order to take her to the nursing office. She was already starting to lose a lot of color, and her lips were turning blue. Hopefully, she wouldn't succumb to hypothermia.

Meanwhile, Dr. Toumi directed the shivering students to follow them, likely using his aptitude as an empath to calm them down. All but one seemed to be freezing and terrified. Mr. Wells had noticed her first, since she was dressed atypically in a Roman looking garment. Her fair complexion and white stola made her look like a marble statue come to life, as if she just walked out of the National Gallery of Art. As he set the girl down on one of the beds, he realized the peculiarity of the other students as well. He hadn't recognized any of them, and he definitely should have known the girl before him, who would have been old enough to have taken one of his classes. Neither were their uniforms quite right.

"Henry," addressed Dean Schulz, breaking his stream of consciousness. "We'll need to start warming her up. Michael had tried a cryogenic spell on her, and she absorbed it."

Mr. Wells joined his two colleagues, forming a heated atmosphere around the teenage girl. Sometimes he forgot how talented his boss was at physical magic since he didn't often see him use it. One of the nurses, Nurse Hargraves, brought a bottle of firejack.

"Really, Rebecca?" questioned Dean Schulz, without losing track of the heating spell.

"Say what you want, but it does have magical enchantments that heat up the body. Otherwise, I would have to drive all the way into Winterburg to pick up the right elixir," she explained, but Dean Schulz still looked at her skeptically. "We're already in big trouble with the USDM, what's a shot of firejack going to do?"

"Alright," acquiesced the dean with a heavy sigh, then signalling for the spell to be halted.

Nurse Hargraves tapped various points on the girl's body, casting a spell that Mr. Wells was unfamiliar with. Suddenly, the girl woke up and the nurse directed her to drink the glass. There was no coughing or dizziness or anything that revealed discomfort on the girl's face. In fact, with trembling fingers, she asked for another shot, and the nurse obliged. Afterwards, she laid back down, and fell asleep with more pink in her cheeks.

"That should be good for now," continued Nurse Hargraves. "I'll get more ingredients and medicines from Winterburg tomorrow. Hopefully, it will stop snowing by then."

"What about the other students?" asked Dean Schulz. "They're with Luke, have you checked on them?"

Just as he said that, Dr. Toumi exited his office and approached the group with a book in his hands.

"What do you have a yearbook for?" asked Mr. Campbell. "Did you identify the students?"

"Oh, yes," he said with a raised voice, handing the vintage tome to Dean Schulz, who let out an even more exasperated sigh.

"Are they who I think they are?" he asked slowly, and Dr. Toumi slowly nodded his head.

"Well?" pushed Mr. Campbell, who seemed to still have a little bit of adrenaline in his veins.

All Dean Schulz did before entering Dr. Toumi's office was turn around and hand the yearbook for Mr. Wells and Mr. Campbell to see. *1969-1970.*

"Well, it seems that the magical community has solved at least one mystery tonight," said Mr. Wells, who had experienced weirder things, and he left the book for Mr. Campbell to read.

EPILOGUE 2: THE COLLEEN

The icy waves of Donegal Bay bit at Aisling's ruddy skin, and the sand beneath her crawled all over her body. Her hair was greasy, and the smell of salt bit her nose. She struggled to get up, being disoriented from all the traveling she had done in the past few hours - from the sunset setting of the Christmas Market to the ambient lighting of the labyrinthine Archives to the dark beach of... *Ireland?* Despite wanting to lay down forever, Aisling was unable to stop herself from getting to her feet.

Aisling didn't know where exactly she was going, but she was headed towards the rocky part of the beach. It was painful to step over the hard stones, but Aisling didn't have far to go. She entered the cave to find a tall, pale woman waiting for her.

"My feet hurt," complained Aisling.

"You'll get used to it," said the woman, uncaring.

"You can't do this to me! This is possession. It's against the law!"

"Human laws don't apply to me. Besides, you signed a contract with me, and you broke it by getting me involved in your little... thing."

"Yeah, but I said I wasn't willing to do anything illegal!"

"Except you were, and I'm the one doing the possession, not you. Besides, your laws and our laws aren't the same. I'm not breaking any laws of my own. Furthermore, haven't you broken several mortal laws already? Don't be a hypocrite. You are condemned by your own standard. Come."

Aisling followed the faerie deep into the cave, ashamed of her own situation. It was pitch black, but she didn't have to worry about where to go since she was possessed. Eventually, Aisling started hearing sounds - a raucous of debauchery. Hysterical laughing, wild screams, and manic shouts came from below.

"Are we going into the Otherworld?" asked Aisling, afraid that the environment she was about to find herself in would be much worse than if she had let herself be arrested by Detective Christie.

"Quiet," ordered the fae, and Aisling found that she could no longer open her mouth to speak.

About the Author

Originally from Virginia, Stephen Sterling is a writer with a background in mathematics. *The Boy Trapped in Time* is his sequel following the events of his debut novel, *The Witch from the Woods.* Inspired by the fantasy novels of his youth, his goal was to weave together mystery, spirituality, and rich interpersonal dynamics within the enchanting setting of a magical school. Outside of writing, Stephen enjoys learning new languages, a passion that often finds its way into his stories, exercising, hiking, and playing with his beloved dogs: Poppy, Palla, and Charlie.

Connect with Stephen Sterling:

Instagram: @stephensterling777

X: @SSterling777

E-mail: stephensterling777@gmail.com

www.ingramcontent.com/pod-product-compliance
Lightning Source LLC
LaVergne TN
LVHW091257150826
845673LV00006B/1449